DADDY'S GREAT ESCAPE

FUNNY CAPERS DOWNUNDER
BOOK 2

JOHN MARTIN

CONTENTS

1. Swimming for his life 1
2. You're not from around here? 4
3. But you don't understand 6
4. Rattling the swear jar 10
5. Meet your new shipmates 13
6. Chug, chug, snort 15
7. This way and that way 17
8. He never tries that shit with me 19
9. Someone has to gut the fish 21
10. The sleeping giants awake 23
11. You've got this wrong 27
12. Father-to-be's reprieve 29
13. Bon Voyage or So Long Sucker 31
14. Enjoy your rat din-dins 34
15. Glad to be mad 37
16. Walking through the graveyard 41
17. A surprise feast 43
18. Who could that be? 46
19. Davy didn't make it 51
20. No one's getting off this island 55
21. He's gotta be fish food by now 56
22. Rubber duckies to the rescue 59
23. But I saw him drown 61
24. Glow of the dead 64
25. Cooking candles 65
26. Last will and testament 67
27. Can you point the way? 69
28. The Three Pallbearers 71
29. My gun is bigger than your gun 73
30. Where'd they go? 75
31. Best mailman I ever had 77
32. No, no, not that 79
33. Screams from above 81
34. Good things happen in the dark 83
35. Sons of peaches 86
36. Out with the rats and snakes 90

37. And stay out until you're dead   92
38. Death watch   95
39. The Great Unwashed   97
40. So you're not dead!   100
41. Dead ducks   102
42. Love me knot   104
43. Reptile stew   107
44. Chitty chitty boong boong   109
45. Quiet as a graveyard   112
46. Figured it out, have you?   115
47. Maria will never know   118
48. They can't make me go, can they?   121
49. A rock show   123
50. Put. Me. Down.   124
51. Whitey's dead   126
52. Revisiting a dead-end job   129
53. Dig it   131
54. Dead buggers can't be choosers   133
55. Keeper of lost soles   135
56. Back from the dead   138
57. A man's gotta have some vices   140
58. I've already got some   142
59. William Clarin stands up   144
60. We just want to go home   146
61. If I say run, ruuuunnn   148
62. Two human popsicles inside a yellow raft   151
63. The ghost of Christmas pasta   153
64. I've just gotta get a message to you   156
65. Do you give up?   157
66. Festive gold-painted coconuts   160
67. 'I'm dreaming of a Whitey Christmas.'   162
68. Bringing home the beacon   164
69. Submerged treasure   166
70. Let me in, you old weasel   169
71. Who are you calling greedy?   170
72. Looking down the barrel again   172
73. I'd bring back the cat o'nine tails for people like him   174
74. Breathe in, breathe out   177
75. I'm coming Maria, I'm coming   180
76. Forked and far from home   181
77. He's a lying old bugger   183
78. You said you could mend it   185

79. You're next, skipper   187
80. Is it just me? Or has this bench gotten shorter?   188
81. They're back   189
82. Rush the house? We're very big on Occupational Health
    and Safety   192
83. We're trained for siege situations like this   194
84. Cave-in   196
85. Pink and black helicopter with white blotches   198
86. Bury me good and deep   201
87. Six voices, one moo and a funeral   203
88. Mad to the end, silly old bugger   205
89. Seaman Smith stays behind with the cow   207
90. The British never told us   209
91. Get me to the birth on time   212
    Next in the series   213
    About the Author   215
    Author's note   216

    My books   219

ONE
SWIMMING FOR HIS LIFE

A TATTOOED ARM reached down from the back of the boat. 'Give me your hand, you stupid surfer.'

Ralph was hauled up and dumped face down on the deck.

He spat out a mouthful of sea-water on the black rubber matting, and gasped. 'Am I glad you came along.'

'What were you even thinking?' the voice above him snapped. 'You should know better at your age! You're more likely to be ripped apart by a White Pointer than catch a good wave in this bay.'

When Ralph lifted his head, the first thing he saw was the gruff man's yellow rubber boots.

When he rolled over, he saw lots of cray pots, nets and hooks. Then he spied a wheelbarrow further up the fishing boat.

The tattooed man's yellowness didn't end with his rubber boots. He was wearing yellow rubber trousers that went all the way to his armpits. He had muscular arms like Popeye, but they were much more heavily tattooed than simple anchors.

Water dripped from Ralph's clothes as he got on to his knees. As he staggered to his feet, the whistle around his neck swung and glinted in the sun before flopping back on to the front of his soggy red-and-black striped shirt. The man facing him had the beginnings of a beard, and he reeked of fish.

Ralph pointed to the shore, which was getting smaller. 'I'm not a bloody surfer! Can't you see I'm a referee? I was chased into the bay by a mob who were unhappy with one of my decisions.' He pointed with a trembling finger. 'If I hadn't swum from the soccer field at the edge of the bay there, I'd probably be dead now.'

The boat was leaving the shelter of the bay. The wind was freshening and waves were becoming bigger. Ralph grabbed a rail as the boat rocked and rolled.

Popeye stooped down and picked up a towel, which he threw at Ralph so he could dab his face dry. Ralph should have looked at it first though. Dried fish entrails taste terrible and the taste just gets worse as they rehydrate. He clenched his eyes shut and made a raspberry sound as he blew through his lips.

The shock of his hand being gripped made him open his eyes and remove the towel from his line of vision.

Popeye smiled as he squeezed Ralph's hand like it was some kind of pain-threshold test, and he shouted above the wind and the chug of the engine. 'You'll get used to swallowing a few fish guts. I'm Davy.'

'Ralph.' He was glad when his hand was released, and he saw he still had all his fingers.

Davy was about his age (the wrong side of thirty) and height (only two or three inches short of six foot) but with hands the size of buckets.

'You're come aboard *The Good Lady*.' Davy began to laugh. 'The skipper's wife thinks he named this tub after her.'

'I won't tell her otherwise. If you just take me back to shore, I'll be on my way.' When he saw that Davy's facial expression had turned dark again, Ralph added hastily: 'Of course, I'll pay you for your troubles.'

Davy spat over the side. 'It ain't up to me. I'm just the lead deckhand on this trawler. You'll have to talk to the skipper.'

Davy pointed to a raised cabin. 'You'll find Hendrik in the wheelhouse, but I've never known him to go back so soon. We usually only return when we have a full load of fish in the hold.'

'How long does that take?'

'Depends. Could be as much as two or three weeks.'

'I can't wait that long!' Ralph cried. 'People will be worried about me.'

Davy spat again. This time his green phlegm teetered on the top of the rail. Ralph didn't have to stare at it for long because a wave crashed up and swept it away.

Davy shrugged. 'Hendrik has a two-way radio in the wheelhouse, which means he can tell the authorities on shore you're safe. Sooner or later he's going to have to do the same for our two other hitchhikers.'

Ralph stretched his eyes wide: 'You mean I'm not the only one?'

TWO
YOU'RE NOT FROM AROUND HERE?

AS RALPH SQUELCHED his way to the wheelhouse, he rehearsed in his head what he was going to say.

The first clue that something funny was going on was when he spotted Hendrik's grinning face as he approached the wheelhouse door.

The skipper opened the door and motioned for Ralph to come in.

The engine was labouring away, but it was quieter in this cramped space though it stank of fish *and* diesel.

The skipper was a large man in his mid-40s with a leathery face. He looked down at Ralph's outfit and laughed. 'The hoodlums have been at it again, haven't they?'

Ralph took a deep breath, then let it out slowly. 'You're not surprised you haven't picked up a surfer?'

Hendrik continued grinning as he steered into the white caps. 'I just don't know why they don't build a big net at the end of the ground?'

'This has happened before?'

'It happens almost every year. If the supporters don't like how the grand final is going for their team, they just remove the goals at one end and chase the referees into the bay.'

Ralph was speechless. He looked down at his black running shoes and saw one of them had got also picked up a stowaway: a small string of green seaweed.

'Let me guess?' the skipper said. 'You're not from around here? They never are.'

Ralph nodded. He worked far down the New South Wales coast but running the line on a soccer field was his way of forgetting the pressures of his real job. Little had he known what was ahead of him when he was told he had been selected to officiate in the final at a little town he barely knew existed.

But the selectors *knew*! If it happened like this every year, of course they had to know. What did that make him? Expendable?

'You need to take me back,' Ralph said. 'I'm expected to cover the mayor's birthday party tonight.'

'Mayor Jim Jones? He had his birthday weeks ago.'

'No, not your mayor, our mayor down the coast. His 50th.'

Hendrik frowned.

'I'm a newspaper reporter. Ralph Whistler. I can't possibly be out here for two or three weeks.'

Hendrik laughed again. 'Who told you we'd be out that long?'

'Your deckhand did.'

'He must have misheard me.' Hendrik blasted him with a sigh of exhaled air. 'If it wasn't for me getting people to help him, I don't know how we'd ever catch anything. He's more of a dickhead than a deckhand!'

'So he's wrong?'

'He never listens. My missus says she doesn't want to see us back for at least six weeks. And she says not to come back at all unless we bring home a couple of crays for Christmas. She makes the best cray-fish pasta.'

THREE
BUT YOU DON'T UNDERSTAND

RALPH SUDDENLY REALISED that missing the mayor's birthday party was the least of his worries.

It was November 11. His first-born child was due to arrive on December 25 and he had been in training to be in the birthing suite to hold his wife's hand.

Ralph rubbed a hand across the back of his neck. 'Six weeks! I'll miss the birth of my daughter!'

Hendrik didn't even turn. Ralph was not sure what he thought the boat might run into. All he could see ahead was water. 'When?' Hendrik said.

'She's due on Christmas Day.'

The skipper kept looking straight ahead and spoke in a deadpan voice. 'How can you possibly know what date the baby will come?'

'Maria's doctor calculated it.'

'And you even know it's going to be a girl!' Hendrik's face formed a smirk. 'Tell me another one!'

'It's true. They can tell these days from the ultrasound.'

The skipper glanced down at the control panel. 'Technology! Figures. I wouldn't have believed years ago the equipment we've got today to help us find where the fish are.'

'So you'll turn round?'

'I'm sure your little lady will be fine without you. All my kids were born when I was at sea. It helps our women-folk to become resilient, and the benefits for us blokes are immense.' He prodded his chest. 'Five kids, and I never had to change one nappy! Not many men can say that!'

'But you don't understand. Maria will be worried.'

'Won't her mother be there to help?'

'Maria's mother lives in Portugal!'

Hendrik turned and squeezed Ralph's shoulder. 'I'm sure your little lady will be all right. You've got other female friends, right?'

Ralph pinched the bridge of his nose. 'If it's about money, I'm happy to pay for the inconvenience of taking me back to port.'

Hendrik stared straight ahead again and gave him a deadpan answer. 'It's not about the money.'

'Is it about the crayfish? I'd happily buy your wife a couple of those.'

He turned around and glared at Ralph as if he were offended.

'What then? What do I have to do for you to take me back?'

He looked ahead again. 'Nothing you can do.'

'But Maria will be worried, and I have work commitments.' Ralph suddenly remembered he had parked his car in a pay zone. 'If my car is still parked outside the soccer ground on Monday morning, it's likely to get towed away.'

Hendrik shrugged. 'I wouldn't worry about that. I'm the only tow-truck driver in town.'

'But you're a fisherman!'

'Only during the fishing season. For the rest of the time I'm a tow-truck driver. Anyway, if I were you, I'd be more worried about what those soccer hooligans are doing to your car right now. The traffic wardens can hardly fine you if the ratbags have pinched the wheels and torched the rest.'

'See why you have to take me back?' Ralph said. 'I beg you.'

Hendrik's voice became loud and angry. 'You don't understand, do you? Do you really think it was just dumb luck that we picked you up?'

Ralph felt the blood drain from his face. 'What are you saying?'

'I told you. This happens nearly every grand final day. If I get the timing right, you can bet your bottom dollar that I can pick up a prospective deckhand on the way out of port.'

Ralph had had enough. He put the whistle into his mouth and blew it as loudly as he could. The sound ricochetted around the metal and glass walls.

Hendrik covered his ears with his hands. When the noise was over, he pointed a finger at Ralph. 'Do that again, and we'll be tossing that whistle overboard with you attached!'

'How else am I supposed to get the message across that I'm a linesman, not a deckhand?'

Hendrik shrugged. 'Do you know how hard it is to find deckhands these days?' He nodded towards Davy who was now stacking cray pots badly on the other side of the window. 'See what I have to put up with? His mother must have dropped him on his head when he was a baby.'

'Davy told me you already had two other blokes aboard.'

'Yes, but goodness knows what condition they'll be in when they wake up and realise they're surrounded by water. They'd have no memory of even leaving the pub last night.'

'It must be nearly 4pm. Wouldn't they be awake by now?'

'With the mickey I slipped them?' He glared at Ralph. 'And don't go getting any ideas about trying to wake them! I don't want any land in sight when they surface.'

'Won't the two of them be enough? Surely you don't want the crew tripping over each other.'

Hendrik looked ahead again. 'I know one of them knows his way around a boat, but the other bloke didn't look much like a fishermen last night.'

'What am I? Some kind of insurance?'

The skipper sounded exasperated. 'If this turns out to be a good trip, what I pay you will be more than enough to cover the board and keep I'll charge you.'

FOUR
RATTLING THE SWEAR JAR

RALPH POINTED to the panel with the dials and knobs. 'Can you at least use that thing to ask them to send a police boat out to get me?'

'Keep your hair on. You haven't had much to do with boats, have you?'

'What makes you say that?'

'Hang on.' Hendrik wrapped his fingers around the wheel as they crashed into a big wave, and the fishing boat lurched violently. The jolt sent Ralph staggering from one side of the little wheelhouse to the whitewashed wall on the other side.

'Fuck,' he said when he had recovered his balance. His right hand stung after he had banged it on the iron wall. 'Fuck, fuck, fuck.' He bent over and buried his hand in his armpit.

When he looked up, Hendrik was shaking a jar of coins in front of his face.

'You can't be serious?' Ralph said.

'No-one swears here without paying up.'

'I thought all you fishermen swore like troopers.'

Hendrik shook the jar again. It was about a third full. 'Come on, cough up. I counted four swear words so that will be four dollars.'

Ralph knew he didn't have any money on him. His wallet was in the back pocket of his trousers that had been hanging on a hook in the locker back at the soccer ground. But he went through the motions of patting his pockets, and then extracting the only things he could find: a soggy red card, a soggy yellow card and a soggy handkerchief. 'That's all I've got.'

'Don't think I won't take this out of your wages?'

'You still don't get it, do you? I have no intention of being press-ganged into your service.'

'You're going to have to work on your balance if you want to be a deckhand.'

'You're not listening!'

Hendrik pointed to the side of the wheelhouse. 'That wall stopped you from flying into the ocean. You won't have that safeguard out on the deck. Even if I see you fall overboard, there's no guarantee I'll double-back to get you. You might be so useless, you're not worth saving.'

Hendrik broke into a smile. 'Heaven knows how you're going to cope using our *au-natural* toilet?'

Ralph's jaw dropped.

Hendrik laughed. 'Everyone gets embarrassed that first time they have to drop their trousers at the stern in front of everyone, but you'll get used to it.'

Ralph continued to glare because he didn't see what was funny. 'I have no intention of shitting off the side of this boat.'

'You're a slow learner. The stern is at the back of the boat.' The laugh lines on Hendrik's face shifted to scowling lines, and he rattled the jar again. 'And that's another dollar out of your wages. Anyway, you'll have to go sooner or later. You can't hold it in for six whole weeks. People have tried and failed, and it's always worse for them in the end.'

The boat ploughed into another big wave, but this time Ralph was already hanging on to the grab rail on the inside of the door. 'Can't you go around those big waves!'

The look Hendrik gave Ralph suggested he thought he was really cuckoo.

'Do yourself a favour.' Ralph pointed. 'Get on that thing. Speak to the authorities.'

Hendrik shook his head. 'I can't do that?'

'Why can't you do that?'

'That's an echo sounder.' Hendrik pointed to a microphone mounted on the ceiling above his head. 'That's the two-way radio. You really don't know anything about boats, do you?' He took a deep breath and exhaled noisily, then muttered. 'Davy's going to have his work cut out trying to make a competent deckhand out of you.' He looked up at the roof. 'Lordy, what are the odds of having two blokes aboard who are as thick as two short planks!'

'What is it about this you are not getting?' Ralph's voice rose. 'I'm a journalist. Unless you get me off this boat pronto, I'm going to use every contact I have in the wider media to expose you.'

'Are you threatening me?' Hendrik shouted back. 'If I hadn't rescued you, you'd be five pieces inside the belly of a shark by now. You owe me. You should be writing nice things about me.'

Ralph held out one open palm. He would have held out two but he saw the big wave coming and felt the need to keep holding tight to the rail. 'Look, I am grateful. I really am. But I just want to go home. I want people I love to know I am safe. I want to sleep in my own bed tonight. Call the police boat. I'm begging you for the last time.'

'Sorry, but I can't do that. It's a duty of care thing. When those other two blokes wake up, they mightn't be so enthusiastic they're bobbing around in all this water. But I know for a fact they'll be happy the police are no where near them.'

The crash of the wave made a mighty sound, which was just as well. If Hendrik had heard Ralph's retort, the new arrival would be even further in the red.

FIVE
MEET YOUR NEW SHIPMATES

HENDRIK DID RELENT A BIT. He said when they arrived at the fishing grounds, he would radio authorities and at least tell them Ralph was safe and well.

'That's something, I suppose,' Ralph said.

'The bad news is it'll take us 12 hours to get to the fishing grounds.' Hendrik smirked. 'The worse news for you is they won't send a rescue boat that far.'

'How can you be sure?'

'Maybe if your name was Harold Holt!'

Hendrik must have noticed Ralph's watery eyes because he put his big arm around his shoulder. 'Why don't you go ask Davy to show you to your cabin? You'll feel better after a sleep.'

'You mean I have my own cabin?'

'Sure, if you don't mind kipping in the engine room. Otherwise you'll be sharing with me and Davy. And our other guests, Darkey and Whitey.'

'Is that their names? Seriously?'

Hendrik ran a hand over his hair. 'Darkey used to crew for me way back when. I assume he met Whitey while they were doing time. I could be wrong though. I know better than to ask too many questions in *The Sailor's Arms.'*

SIX
CHUG, CHUG, SNORT

DAVY LIFTED A HATCH, and they climbed down five rungs of a ladder to reach the cramped, airless cabin.

A low-voltage globe in the corner threw out a little light.

Two sets of bunks came into focus.

The two men with an aversion to the police were sleeping in the two bottom bunks. The racket was deafening! The engine room was obviously on the other side of the wall. *Chug, chug, chug, snort, chug, chug, chug, groan, chug, chug, chug, belch, chug, chug, chug, fart.*

Ralph turned to leave. 'I can't sleep in here. There's not even a porthole.'

Davy turned him around by gripping his shoulder.

'Trust me. You wouldn't want a leaky porthole when you're below the waterline.'

'Hendrik mentioned the engine room?'

Davy grinned. At least, Ralph think he grinned. It was hard to see in this light. 'The last man who slept there wears a hearing aid now!'

Ralph looked over to the snoring shapes. 'When do you think they'll wake up?'

Davy shrugged. 'I hope they wake up before we reach the fishing grounds, otherwise me and you will be busy.'

He opened a cupboard tucked in the corner. 'You'll find your work clothes in here.' He pointed to a cupboard under a bottom bunk. 'Rubber boots are down there. You should find a pair to fit you.'

SEVEN
THIS WAY AND THAT WAY

RALPH FELT like a canary in this clobber. They stood on the back deck, both dressed in ridiculous yellow rubber bibs and jackets.

'You need to quit calling this the back,' Davy said when Ralph asked him why they were standing there. 'This is the stern.' He pointed to the left. 'That's port-side.' He scratched his head, then pointed to the right and said hesitantly: 'Or maybe that's port-side. Whatever. Starboard is whatever the other side isn't. Get that?'

Ralph nodded half-heartedly. Surely, it would be less confusing just to say left and right and front and back. Then again, he wondered if Davy knew his left from right either.

Davy pointed up front. 'The sharp bit is definitely the bow. I know that's right.'

'I really don't think I'm going to be much help to you.'

'You mightn't have a choice if those blokes don't wake up. There's too much work for one bloke to do.'

Ralph felt the blood drain from his face. 'What do you mean not wake up? You mean . . . die?'

Davy shrugged. 'It happens.'

Ralph opened his eyes wide.

'One bloke died only last year. In the bunk you're in, matter of fact.'

'My bunk?'

'Yeah, we don't usually use it now on account of its smell. He was asleep for two days before we twigged he was dead and bunged him in the freezer with the catch until we needed the room for more fish. Then we put him back in his bunk for the return voyage. You have no idea how hard it was getting him up and down the ladder. Bugger wouldn't bend.'

'Don't tell me?' Ralph said. 'He was another drunkard your boss befriended in *The Sailor's Arms*, and spiked his drink.'

'Wrong! I pulled him out of the bay during last year's soccer grand final. He threw up all over the deck when I hauled him aboard, and I put him straight to bed. The coroner found he choked on his own whistle during the night.'

EIGHT
HE NEVER TRIES THAT SHIT WITH ME

RALPH COULD SEE Davy was sizing him by the way he looked him up and down. 'How much do you reckon you can lift?'

Ralph shrugged. 'I normally have no problem picking the newspaper up off the lawn.'

'Are you shitting me?'

'Shhhhh. You don't want the man with the swear jar to hear that kind of language.'

'You know about the jar then? Do you know all the coins in there, he's put in himself. It's drinking money his wife doesn't know about.'

'Is it?' Ralph squinted at him.

'He never tries that shit with me.' Davy spat over the back, er, stern. Or perhaps he sternly spat. 'I don't think he trusts himself to be down here on deck anyway. Hendrik's got two left feet and two left hands, so it's better he stays out of the way and does what he does best, which is steering the boat to where the fish are at.'

He spat again. 'But seriously? How much can you lift?'

'Hmm, I can only measure it in pounds. Two pounds of carrots? Three pounds of potatoes?'

Ralph detected a look of disgust.

'Look,' Ralph said. 'I don't want to be here at all. I have a pregnant wife, I'm expected to cover the mayor's birthday tonight, goodness knows what state my car is in now and I was nearly murdered today.'

'Aren't you being a bit of a drama queen?'

'What!' Ralph pointed towards the wheelhouse. 'Your skipper not only refuses to take me back to port, he refuses to even radio in that I'm safe and sound.'

'Worse things happen at sea.' Davy laughed at what he obviously thought was a pretty good joke. Then he studied Ralph with more serious intent. 'Thing is, if those blokes don't wake up, you and I will be pushing shit uphill. I can probably manage the winch and the nets and the lines and the pots and baiting what needs to be baited, but you're going to have to carry the fish to the cool room.'

'On my own!'

'You won't have to carry them far, for fuck's sake.' He pointed to the wheelbarrow halfway down the boat. 'Just pour them in there.'

'Oh, that's what that's for!'

Davy gave Ralph an odd look. 'Not the wheelbarrow, you dork! That's only for carrying sleepers aboard!'

He walked forward (or maybe it was aft), past the wheelbarrow, and picked up a big red plastic tub from a pile of tubs.

'This is what you use. When these babies are full, they only weigh about forty pounds. If we get among a good school, you'll probably be going back and forth for a good eight hours.'

NINE
SOMEONE HAS TO GUT THE FISH

DAVY SAID he had worked with Darkey Johnstone, so he knew the man knew what he was doing. If the other bloke was even half as competent that had to make him at least twice as good as Ralph.

Ralph knew he meant this as a putdown, but what did he care?

'If they do wake up, we'll put you on light duties,' Davy said.

'You'd do that?'

Davy grinned. 'Well, someone has to gut the fish.'

'What?'

'And do the cooking.'

'I thought you said *light* duties?'

'Well, you do have experience. Good thing I brought carrots and potatoes aboard. I know now you'll be able to lift them on your own.'

Ralph's voice became shrill. 'Maria does 99 per cent of our cooking for a good reason. I think you'd soon tire of me working in the kitchen long before six weeks is up!'

'Galley,' Davy corrected him. 'And it'll be three weeks tops.'

'That's not what Hendrik told me! He said his wife doesn't want to see him back in port until Christmas.'

Davy went pale. 'I wondered why he had so much food for me to bring aboard. I left at least half of it back at the co-op.'

Ralph tut-tutted. 'He's not going to be happy.'

'Maybe not, but at least he'll have more room for fish.'

'That's one good thing then. I like eating fish, I'm just not so sure how well I'll go cooking it.'

'You won't have to stress about it,' Davy said. 'Hendrik doesn't let us touch any of the choice bits of the catch. That means you're going to have to come up with lots of different recipes for fish heads and fish guts.'

TEN
THE SLEEPING GIANTS AWAKE

DARKEY DID WAKE up in the middle of the night. So did his mate.

Ralph knew this because just when he was finally drifting off to sleep, they turned on the light, and found a packing box they put on its side and wedged between the bunks so they could play cards.

Instinct told Ralph to keep pretending to be asleep. It took only a few minutes listening to them to tell these weren't the kind of men who'd take kindly to being told to keep the noise down. One of them had an annoying sniff.

Ralph had to resist screaming out when he heard one of them strike a match, but the cocktail of gases in the room didn't explode as he had feared. The cigarette smoke just made the cabin smell more suffocating.

Ralph had no idea if Davy was also pretending to be asleep.

Ralph, of course, had the bunk that smelt of dead man and dead fish, and Davy was hot-bedding it with Hendrik, who did the night-shift steering the boat. At daylight, the plan was for them to switch around for a few hours.

That's how Ralph knew it was dawn when Darkey's and Whitey's card game ended.

A sliver of daylight came through the hatch before Hendrik came down the ladder.

Both Davy and Ralph sat up in their bunks in time to see Hendrik screwing up his face as he breathed in the fetid, smoke-filled air.

Ralph could see the two other men below clearly now.

'Hello Darkey.' Hendrik nodded to the enormous bald man. 'Nice to have you onboard again. Didn't you remember there's a rule here against gambling? You're just lucky I haven't got my jar with me.'

Darkey looked across to Whitey. 'Don't fall for that money-in-the-jar shit.'

Hendrik sat down on the end of one of the bottom bunks and started removing his boots. 'Did you boys sleep well?'

Darkey glared. 'We slept pretty well before the noise of the engine woke us up. I thought you were going to sound-proof this cabin? Isn't it about time you rolled back some of your profits into upgrading this rust bucket?'

One of Hendrik's boots rolled on to the floor with a clunk. 'The money's just not there any more to pay for fancying the sleeping quarters up.'

Darkey looked across to Whitey. 'Don't believe that bullshit either. You're looking at one of the richest men on the coast.'

Whitey sniffed. So *he* was the culprit! He was thinner than Darkey but his knees were up near his chin on that low chair. He had unkempt long hair, which made him look like a hairy spider.

Off went Hendrik's second boot. Another clunk. 'Why does the ambience worry you anyway?'

Ralph saw Davy scratch his head. It was unfair to use a word like *ambience* in his presence.

Hendrik stood back up and started unbuttoning his coat. 'Don't you remember telling me you needed to lie low.' He opened his palms. 'Well, here you are! Miles from anyone!'

'I don't recall telling you anything?' Darkey sounded like he had bile rising in his mouth. 'Tell you what I think? I think you've been up to your old tricks again. You slipped something in our drinks.'

'What? And carried you down the gangplank? You think I'm that strong?'

'I don't remember arriving here. Explain that?'

Hendrik took off his trousers and looked up towards Davy. 'Scram, you. Thanks for warming the bed.'

Ralph yelled: 'Wait! Who's steering the boat?'

'Relax,' Hendrik said. 'There are no rocks to hit out here. Davy will be up in the wheelhouse in a jiffy.' He looked up again. 'Move your arse.'

'And Davy knows how to operate the radio?' Ralph said.

'Radio?'

'You said once we're at the fishing grounds, you'd radio and tell people I was OK.'

Hendrik chortled. 'I did, didn't I?'

He looked over to Darkey and Whitey. 'My apologies, boys. You haven't met this joker yet, have you? Let me introduce Ralph Whistler, ace newspaper reporter.'

Hendrik's grin widened.

'I'd better come clean, Ralph. Truth No. 1: we still have a couple of hours to reach our destination. Truth No. 2: The radio frequency won't travel all the way back to shore anyway.'

Ralph blinked back tears. 'You know how important this is to me! Why would you lie?'

Hendrik shrugged. 'I could still radio a ship in the vicinity to come pick you up. No telling where they'd take you though. Japan. Panama.'

Everyone else laughed. Then Whitey leaned over the table and started whispering into Darkey's ear. That didn't look good.

By now, Davy had slid down from the top and was waiting for Darkey and Whitey to shift the packing case. Hendrik climbed up from the end of the bed. 'Come on, scram you lot. I need some kip.'

He looked over to Ralph and said: 'Davy will show you where the galley is. Don't burn my bacon. I'll be up and about again in an hour.'

Ralph quickly dressed back into his referee's gear and followed Davy, Darkey and Whitey up the ladder

Whitey was about 10 years younger than Darkey. Both of them had to stoop to cross the cabin but Whitey stooped the most.

What Darkey gave away in height, he more than made up for in heft. He had an ear-ring, like a modern-day pirate.

They both had similar-shaped scars on their cheeks, like they had got one of those buy-one-get-one-free deals.

As Ralph followed Whitey up the ladder he realised both men were holding threatening objects in their hands.

ELEVEN
YOU'VE GOT THIS WRONG

RALPH THOUGHT about backing back down the ladder.

But the bellowing voice of the skipper reminded him he didn't want to be down there either. 'Make sure you shut that hatch. If I have to get up to close it …'

This made Ralph hesitate but he decided the devils you don't know are better than the one you do.

Turns out, he was wrong!

As Ralph climbed slowly through the hatch, Whitey was pointing his gun straight at his head. Darkey had a big spanner he must have pinched from the engine room in the middle of the night.

'It's like this, reporter.' Whitey sniffed. Didn't the man have a handkerchief? 'You're a risk we don't want to take. You might blow our cover.'

Ralph put his hands up. 'Who am I going to tell out here?' He started blabbering. 'Even if I had a way of filing copy, my tin-pot newspaper wouldn't be remotely interested. We don't even cover the law courts any more. We only do cheque presentations and the mayor's birthday party. I'm not going to tell anyone about you blokes. Honestly.'

'We don't do honest,' Darkey said.

It was about now Ralph he was alone with the baddies. 'W-what have you done with Davy?'

Darkey smiled. 'Surprising how easy it is to push a bloke over-board when they're not expecting the shove. A shark is probably licking his lips by now.'

Ralph looked out on the becalmed sea and wondered why the boat was still rolling. Then he worked it out: his trembling was the culprit.

Both hoods started laughing.

'You should see the look on your face.' Darkey slapped Ralph on the back. He wiped tears from his eyes. 'I can't believe you'd think we'd throw Davy overboard. He has just gone ahead to the wheelhouse.'

Whitey was no longer smiling and he was still pointing the gun at Ralph. He sniffed, like he was trying to stop his brains from leaking out of his nose. Then he dropped his voice.

'The thing is, Davy knows how to drive this boat. But you? I reckon you *will* have to get off.'

Ralph gulped. Even though he had been trying to get off this boat since he had got on it, he certainly didn't fancy taking another swim.

TWELVE
FATHER-TO-BE'S REPRIEVE

WHITEY FROGMARCHED RALPH UP to the wheelhouse, with Darkey in tow.

Davy must have seen what was happening. But he was still surprised when the door swung open. 'What do you think you're doing?'

Whitey pointed the gun at Davy. 'Out of there.'

'But who's going to steer the boat?' Davy raised his hands and stepped out.

'Darkey is perfectly capable.'

The bald man nodded and pushed past Davy.

But instead of taking the wheel, he began smashing the radio with his spanner.

'Hey,' Davy said. 'We might need that.'

'Can't take the risk,' Whitey said. 'Your boss said it himself. The radio is useless at the fishing grounds. But we're not there yet, are we?'

Then he waved the gun Ralph's way. 'Which brings us to this problem …'

'I told you. I won't tell.' Ralph was still shaking. 'Who am I going to tell?'

'Damn right,' Whitey said. 'You can't tell anyone if you're dead.'

Darkey came out of the wheelhouse in time to hear that. 'Now hang on. I've done some bad things in my time, but never murder.'

'It wouldn't be murder. If anyone asks, we'd say he decided to go for a swim. It would be our word against, well, nobody's.' He gave Davy a threatening look. 'Maybe you'd like a swim too?'

'Both of them!' Darkey said.

'It's not like they'd ever find their bodies.'

Davy's forehead creased. 'I'm no dobber.' He turned to the bald man and gave him a pleading look. 'You know that.'

'He's right.' Darkey said. 'Davy never squealed on me before. And God knows he's known stuff.'

Whitey tapped the butt of the gun against his cheek. 'Shush. I need a minute to think.'

It was one of the longest minutes of Ralph's life. It gave him lots of time for his life to flash before his eyes. Too much time, if truth be known. He really hadn't wanted to see the DVDs from the anti-natal classes ever again.

Ralph blubbered: 'All I wanted was to see my child be born. Now she'll grow up without a dad.'

Through the prism of his tears, Ralph couldn't really see anyone clearly. He could just feel the wetness on his cheeks and hear the pitter-patter of little teardrops on the deck.

But Darkey's voice was unmistakable.

'I tell you, Whitey, this ain't right. Nobody told me the bloke is a father-to-be.'

He addressed his hostage: 'When's the big due date, Ralph?'

'Christmas Day,' Ralph sobbed.

'Ahhhhh,' Darkey said. 'Just like the Baby Jesus.'

You could almost hear Whitey's eyes rolling. 'Didn't you listen to him? He's having a girl. You have to be a boy to be called Jesus.'

'It doesn't matter.' Darkey pushed Davy gently back towards the wheelhouse. 'Steer a course to Senator Mad Bill's Island.'

THIRTEEN
BON VOYAGE OR SO LONG SUCKER

AS THEY APPROACHED THE ISLAND, Ralph could see it was no bigger than a soccer pitch. Near one end was a large building surrounded by coconut trees. As the boat came closer, a flag-post came into sight. A bit closer and Ralph could see an Australian flag fluttering high above the concrete building, which had small windows.

Davy cut the engine, and stepped out of the wheelhouse. 'I can't go in any closer.' He threw the anchor over the side.

Whitey trained the gun on Ralph again. 'Looks like you're going for a swim after all, journalist boy.'

Now the hum of the engine had gone, they could hear each other clearly.

Keeping the gun aimed at Ralph, Whitey turned his head to Darkey. 'Are you sure this Mad Bill hasn't got a phone?'

'He's just a harmless old hermit. He doesn't have any contact with the outside world.'

Ralph was literally looking down the barrel of a gun, imagining the bullet hurtling out the barrel at more than twice the speed of sound. He really didn't want his last thought on earth to be about Maria and their unborn daughter.

Whitey sniffed up a lungful of air. 'Well, shit, if this bloke ain't got a phone how the bejesus did he become a senator?'

'He's not really a politician.' Darkey laughed. 'He has tried to get elected into the Senate a couple of times but why would anyone vote for him? He doesn't even like most other people. His nickname is a running joke.'

The boat had come to a standstill about 25 yards from the island now, and Ralph could see the building also had a chimney and a small flight of steps leading up to a door.

Whitey frowned. 'How did you even know about this bloke?'

'I thought everyone knew about Senator Mad Bill?'

Whitey sniffed three times, then focussed back on Ralph. 'So are you ready for your swim, journalist boy?'

'Shouldn't we wait for Hendrik to wake up? He was pretty specific he wanted me to cook him some bacon for breakfast.'

'How can you think of his stomach at a time like this?'

That's when Davy came across all sheepish. 'I have a confession to make. The bacon was one of the things I left back at the co-op.'

Darkey's eyes widened. 'No bacon!'

Whitey sniffed again. 'You and your bacon!' He tapped the butt of the gun against his sweaty forehead. 'Maybe we should all go ashore. Perhaps this old man has a supply of bacon.'

Davy said: 'I told you, I can't get in closer. We'd have to lower the rowboat.'

'Good idea,' Ralph said. 'We could all go together, save getting wet.'

'Ain't no point,' Darkey said. 'I told you, no-one ever comes here. So how would he even get bacon? He probably has to eat rats.'

'Rats!' Whitey cried.

'Haven't you heard about the infestation of rats on all these islands out here?' Darkey said. 'I guess the rodents swam from ships that ran on to the rocks. They've evolved to be the size of cats, probably quite meaty.'

'I ain't eating no rat,' Whitey said. He started saying something else but by then he had pushed Ralph over the side by this time and it was hard for him to tell what it was as he tumbled towards the water. It was either "Bon Voyage" or "So Long, Sucker".

FOURTEEN
ENJOY YOUR RAT DIN-DINS

THEY DIDN'T WAIT to see if Ralph would be all right.

As he waded towards the shore, he heard the engine splutter into life and Whitey shout: 'Remember, if the police hear about this we'll know where to find you. Enjoy your rat din-dins!'

When Ralph hauled his dripping body on to the dry rocks, he turned and saw the trawler disappearing. Ralph turned again and surveyed the house. A torn curtain moved in one of the tiny windows upstairs.

He clambered to his feet and headed to the front stairs.

What was this place? It looked like an old concrete fortress. Ralph climbed the short flight of steps and knocked on the big metal door.

No-one answered.

He began knocking more loudly.

Still no answer.

Maybe it had been a trick of the light in the window? Maybe there was no-one here. But why would the door be locked?

He went back down the steps and picked up a fist-sized rock.

He took that back up, and used it as a knocker. Ralph suspected the rock would leave pock marks, but he was wrong. This iron door was obviously built to withstand much more than this force. The rock smashing against the door made a hell of a clang though.

When he heard approaching footsteps, he stopped and put his ear to the door.

That's when he heard a whiny, high-pitched voice. 'I've got a loaded shotgun here, sonny, so you better go back to where you are from if you know what's good for you. I don't want whatever you're selling.'

'I'm not trying to sell you anything.'

'That's what they all say. This island isn't for sale either.'

'I don't want to buy your island. All I want is to use your phone. Or radio. Or whatever it is you use to contact the mainland.'

Everything went quiet. Ralph listened for a few moments but deduced the old man had gone away.

He sat down on the top step and tried to work out what to do next.

Then he realised: what could he do?

Ralph stood up and knocked again.

He heard footsteps again.

The voice returned to the other side of the door. 'Why can't you leave me alone. I don't need encyclopaedias nor vacuum cleaners. I've got everything I need.'

'You don't understand. I need help.'

Ralph guessed the desperation in his voice finally came through.

The door opened a crack, and he felt the old man's eyes on him. Then it opened some more and Ralph could see him. He was about 80 and his ragged jeans were held up with suspenders over his checked shirt. He'd be lucky to be eight stone. He was a step higher than Ralph but he still didn't come up to his neck. He wouldn't have looked threatening at all if he hadn't been pointing a rusty old shotgun up at Ralph's head. 'How do I know you're not one of *them*?' he said.

Not for the first time today, Ralph put up his hands. 'One of who?'

'Them! An Asian or a black man.'

Ralph pointed to his skin and his voice rose. 'Do I look Asian or black?'

'You might have converted.'

'What? That is ridiculous. You can't convert to another skin colour.'

'Michael Jackson did.' The old man used a foot to open the door a bit wider.

'Michael Jackson? How do you know about him? I thought you were supposed to be a hermit?'

'Who told you that?'

'Aren't you Senator Mad Bill?'

'*Don't* call me that.' The gun wobbled, and Ralph hoped the trigger wasn't too sensitive.

'Do you want to put that thing down?'

The old man lowered the gun. 'OK, sonny. But just keep your hands where I can see them.' He squinted. 'What's that thing you've got hanging from your neck?'

'Oh this?' Ralph merely pointed to it, but even that made the old man raise the gun again. 'That's just my whistle, Senator.'

His trigger finger trembled. 'Didn't I tell you not to call me that? As far as I know, I never actually got in, so it disrespects a great democratic institution.' He lowered the gun again and squinted. 'How do I know you're not a commie or a Muslim? Do you have a passport?'

'What? I don't need a passport. This is Australia.'

'Ah, but is it? The British established a military presence on this island in World War II. So who knows who owns it?'

Ralph sighed. 'If you'd like, I can empty my pockets so you can see I'm not armed and I haven't got a passport.'

Ralph reached in and slowly pulled out his once-wet, dry-again, soggy-again red and yellow cards, and his sodden handkerchief. 'These are the only bits of ID I have, sorry.'

The old man pointed the shotgun to the ground and grumbled. 'I suppose you'd better come in.'

FIFTEEN
GLAD TO BE MAD

'I DON'T MIND BEING CALLED Mad Bill, as long as you use the word "mad" in the right sense. I'm angry, not crazy.'

The bewhiskered old man said this as he led Ralph into a khaki-coloured room, which had a series of wanted posters hanging on the peeling walls. Ralph didn't know anyone who was actually wanted (except Darkey and Whitey and he couldn't even be sure about them). But if he had to guess, these posters depicted long-dead Nazis and longer-dead bushrangers. The swastikas and Ned Kelly armour gave it away.

Mad Bill sat in a comfy armchair and motioned for Ralph to sit on a white plastic chair in the corner.

'I'm just mad about what this country has become.' He fixed his eyes on Ralph. 'What did you say your name was again, sonny?'

'I didn't, but it's Ralph. Ralph Whistler.'

'Is that why you are wearing that thing around your neck? So you don't forget your name?'

Ralph held the whistle out in front of him, and laughed. 'It's a long story. You wouldn't believe it.'

'Try me. Time is one of the things I have plenty of.'

Ralph frowned. 'What are the other things?'

'Oh no.' Mad Bill waved a finger at Ralph. 'I'm not giving up my secrets that easily. You first.'

Ralph told him about the soccer game that ended with him being chased into the bay, how he had been picked up by the trawler, threatened at gunpoint and then made to swim to the island. All he wanted to do was get home to his pregnant wife Maria and resume his crappy job.

'Maria? Is she a wop?'

'She's Portuguese.'

'Is she black?'

'What? No … just tanned. Why?'

'I gotta tell you I don't believe in mixed marriages.'

'If I can just use your phone I'll get out of your hair.' Ralph immediately regretted saying this when he realised Mad Bill had probably parted ways long ago with most of the hair on his head except for two grey outcrops. 'I have to let people know I'm safe, better still get someone to come get me.'

'I haven't got a phone, sonny. I can't see the point. I can't think of anyone I'd want to talk to. You're just lucky I had that plastic chair you're sitting on. No way were you going to sit on my upholstered chairs in those wet clothes.'

'You must have *some* means of communication?'

'That's exactly what the chap said who came to the island and tried to sell me some new-fangled thing called a computer and some other thing he called a satellite dish that he claimed could send messages through thin air. Well, I wasn't about to fall for that! I sent him packing after he said I could check just about any fact I could think about on the computer-thingy.' He pointed to the bookshelf. 'How could a little box possibly hold more information than the encyclopaedias I had bought just the week before?'

Ralph's hopes rose. 'So you do get people coming to the island sometimes?'

The old man nodded. 'I'm not as isolated as you might think. The encyclopaedia salesman came just after the vacuum-cleaner salesman.' He pointed to the bookshelf again. 'Did you know Russia has invaded Afghanistan? Bloody commies and Muslims deserve each other.'

'When do you think the next salesman will come around?'

'Hmmm, hard to say.' Mad Bill gazed into space. 'A real estate man does come about once a year. I've seen his boat out the window. He just leaves a note under the door. It always says the same thing.' Clearly, he had committed it to memory. '*I recently sold another property in this very desirable area. Why not let me valuate your property? You might be amazed how much it's worth now.*'

'So when do you next expect to see him?'

'Hard to say. He was only here last week. But you know what salesmen are like? This bugger is so persistent it wouldn't surprise me to see him sooner but if he sticks to schedule I'm going to have another 51 weeks of peace.'

Ralph clenched his eyes shut and tried to gather his thoughts. 'You must have some way to get a message to the mainland?'

'Can't think of any.' When Ralph opened his eyes, the old man was picking his teeth with a wooden toothpick. 'You could always try writing a message out and stuffing it inside a bottle. All kind of interesting things drift past this island. Where'd you think that plastic chair came from? Last year we had a flock of bath-toy ducks float by on the current. My guess is they fell off a container ship. There are probably some confused penguins down in Antarctica right now, not to mention an outdoor setting missing one chair.'

'Is that how you got hold of that toothpick? It fell off the back of a container ship?'

'This?' He offered it to Ralph. 'Nope, I carved this from driftwood. I guess I'll have to share it from now on.'

Ralph waved the toothpick away.

'Please yourself. I'll never cease to understand how a fellow can happily exchange bodily fluids with a foreign woman, yet quibble over sharing a bit of spit with a white man.'

Ralph ignored that comment. 'You don't understand, do you? I have to get off this island. What if you fall ill? You must have flares? Or a beacon? You must have a way of summoning medical help?'

'Nope.' Mad Bill hung his head a little. 'I'm an old man. I just expect to die here.' Then he brightened a little. 'I know I wasn't all that welcoming at first but there's a good side to you coming here. Now I will have someone to bury me.' He hung his head again. 'Shame there'll be no-one here to bury you when you pop off.'

Ralph threw his head back. 'There *must* be a way to get off this island?'

Mad Bill shrugged: 'None that I can think of.'

'Where do you get your mail from?'

'I used to get visits from a mailman, but he hasn't been around in years.'

'What about your food? You must get supplies from somewhere? Fuel for your generator?'

'Nope. I don't have a generator. Only a stove, and I get wood for that at low tide when I can get at a couple of galleons that ran up on the rocks here in the 1800s. I grow my own veggies, and do a bit of fishing on the south-side of the island. If I feel like some meat I go hunting.'

Ralph suddenly felt sick. The old man was talking about hunting for rat, wasn't he? He had been reduced to eating rodents! 'Where's the t-toilet?'

SIXTEEN
WALKING THROUGH THE GRAVEYARD

MAD BILL POINTED TO A DOORWAY. 'Well, the toilet used to be through there.' He shook his head. 'But that dunny stopped working 20 years ago and I nailed some shelves up and turned the room into a pantry. I left the toilet there though and, boy, has it come in handy.'

He saw Ralph screw up his face.

'You can turn your nose up, but I don't know why no-one else has thought about doing the same. You don't need a step-ladder to get to the high shelves, you just have to be careful to put the lid down before you step on it. And that chain comes in really handy for hanging pots.'

Ralph put a hand on his stomach. 'I'd love to hear more but I really, really need to go to the toilet.'

Mad Bill scratched his head. 'Of course. Follow me.'

He walked to the front door, stepping past the shotgun, which was leaning against the wall, and led Ralph down the steps.

At the bottom, he pointed.

'If you walk through the cemetery over there ...'

There was a *cemetery*? Ralph tried not to look shocked. What had the British soldiers been up to on this island that had left some of them dead?

'... you can't miss the big tree ahead of you, which leans over the water.' Mad Bill cackled.

Ralph gulped, and started walking.

The thought of hanging out of a tree and pooping into the Pacific Ocean had an antidiarrheal effect on him as he strode towards the graveyard just 40 or 50 steps away.

A rustic park bench stood in front of four gravestones. Ralph stooped and examined the writing on the headstones. Really? The headstones listed the deaths all in the 1950s, which meant none of the them hadn't occurred during the 1939-'45 war!

Next to the headstones was a ledge, which obviously served as a little shrine. Two burnt-out candles suggested Mad Bill must come here to pay his respects.

When Ralph looked up, he saw the tree up ahead and remembered what Hendrik had said: he couldn't hold it in forever.

As he came closer, he could see the seat wedged between two branch forks that hung over the water. It was amazing what Mad Bill could carve out of driftwood!

He spied a stack of leaves too. Obviously, Mad Bill hadn't perfected paper-making yet.

It was while Ralph was up there on the swaying branches that overhung the water, he heard the gun shot.

Oh shit!

The old man was shooting a rat for dinner!

SEVENTEEN
A SURPRISE FEAST

MAD BILL CAME DOWNSTAIRS WEARING a suit and tie, which made Ralph feel a bit awkward even though his shorts and shirt were now dry.

'Don't worry, you're not the worst-dressed dinner guest I've had here.' The old man looked Ralph up and down in the flickering light. 'I never knew there were such things as tacky vacuum-cleaner costumes until that salesman came around. He sucked up his dinner through a hose.'

Mad Bill led Ralph into the dining room, which was lit by candles.

Ralph pinched his nose. 'What's that smell?'

'You'll get used to the stinky candles in a few years' time.'

The dining table was set up with silver service, candelabras and placemats at either end. The table was so large, Ralph realised it had probably had a very different use during World War 2. He could imagine maps being spread out on it and being pored over by three or four British army officers with monocles.

Ralph could hear something bubbling away in the adjoining kitchen. But hungry as he was, he wasn't sure he could cope with what he knew Mad Bill was going to serve.

The old man told him where to sit.

He brought the dish to the table in a covered serving bowl.

Ralph thought about what was waiting for him under the silver lid.

Would it actually look like a rat looking up at him with its beady little eyes, little pink nose and long whiskers? He felt sweat running down he neck.

Md Bill put the dish down with a flourish.

'Ta-dah.' He lifted the lid to reveal all.

In this light, it looked like long cylindrical chunks in a white sauce.

'Thank goodness,' Ralph blurted. 'You had me going. I really thought you were serving rat.'

Mad Bill cackled. 'I wouldn't eat rat. I'd probably get ratty bits stuck under my dental plate. I can see why you'd think that I might eat rodents though. There are rats everywhere on this island. It's a wonder you didn't trip over them on your way to the tree?'

'I didn't see any.'

'It would be different if you were traipsing over there at night. That's why I keep a piss pot under my bed. The aggressive little buggers mostly seem to come out in the dark.'

'I thought they ran away from people?'

'This lot evolved without the fear of humans being around. When I turned up, they just assumed I was a new item in their food chain.' He eyed Ralph up and down. 'They'd probably think you were an even tenderer morsel.'

He returned to the kitchen and came back with his own plate. He sat down at his end of the table and lifted his cutlery.

'Come on, eat up. This is actually a treat. Let's see if you can guess what it is?'

Ralph poked at the food with his fork. 'Is it zucchini in white sauce?'

Mad Bill cackled. 'You saw my vegetable garden when you arrived then?'

'You have vegetables? Here?'

'Oh yes. If you had gone around the other side of the house, you would have seen my veggie patch.'

'What do you grow?'

'Lettuce, beans, sweet potatoes, zucchinis, cucumbers.'

Ralph felt better about tasting the food now.

He lifted the fork to his mouth and started to chew.

It didn't taste like anything he had ever eaten. Certainly it didn't taste like vegetables. If he had to choose, he'd say it tasted a bit like fish and a bit like chicken at the same time.

'Like it?' Mad Bill wiped his mouth with his napkin.

'I thought you said it was zucchini?'

'I didn't say that. You did.'

Ralph took in another mouthful in the hope he'd be able to pinpoint the taste.

'It's my own recipe. You won't find it in Jamie Oliver's cookbooks.' There he went again. First Michael Jackson, now Jamie Oliver. The man must have found a way to keep up with popular culture somehow.

'When I came here, you wouldn't believe how bad the rat problem was. No wonder people used to die on this island. If they didn't actually have plague when they came here, they probably soon did.'

He waved his fork. 'But I got the rat problem under control. I imported from the mainland a whole lot of tiger snakes to keep them down. Say, you didn't see any snakes on your way to the tree? You wouldn't want to be bitten by a tiger snake out here. I think you'd die a pretty horrible death.'

By this stage, Ralph had stopped eating as the penny dropped.

The good news was that it wasn't rat. The bad news was that he was eating a snake that had *dined* on rat.

EIGHTEEN

WHO COULD THAT BE?

WHAT ELSE COULD RALPH DO? Not only was this his first meal in over a day, he could see Mad Bill had gone to a lot of trouble to provide some protein for his guest.

So Ralph kept plugging away at it.

His mother had actually prepared him for this all those years ago, when she announced with great pride (time and time again) she had a special treat for dinner, and it always turned out to be tripe.

'Let's pretend it's rice custard,' Ralph's sister used to whisper to him when their mother left the room. 'Sooner you eat up, the sooner it'll be over, the happier she'll be that you enjoyed it and the sooner we can have real pudding.'

But this rice-pudding strategy didn't prepare Ralph for what happened next in Mad Bill's dining room.

As soon as the old man saw Ralph had eaten everything but the shotgun pellets he had put to the side of his plate, his eyes lit up.

'There's more in the pot in the kitchen if you like it so much.'

Ralph waved his hands as he forced down the last swallow. 'Delicious! But I couldn't eat another thing. I find if I have too much to eat at night, I have trouble sleeping.'

The truth was his stomach had begun doing somersaults again. He ought to make another trip to the tree. But in the dark! He really hoped the pains would go away.

Mad Bill waved a finger. 'I get it! You want to save it for breakfast, don't you? You want to think all night of the treat to come?'

Ralph smiled weakly. He hoped the flicker of the candles was masking how green he felt.

Mad Bill rose. 'Shall we adjourn to the lounge for drinks then? I've brought some nice sherry up from the tunnels in the basement.'

Ralph gasped as he rose awkwardly from his chair. 'Tunnels?'

'There are two of them down there.'

'Where do they go to? The mainland? Perhaps they're my way out of here?'

'I couldn't tell you where they go,' Mad Bill said. 'I've never been game to venture far past the entrance of either of them.'

Ralph followed Mad Bill to the open door, and the old man pointed to a cracked leather chair in the next room. Thank goodness he wasn't pointing to the uncomfortable white plastic chair.

Ralph sank deeply into the chair, whose springs had seen better days. 'Who built these tunnels? When? Why?'

Mad Bill sat down opposite and shrugged. 'I'm guessing the military in World War 2 built them, but "why" is a whole other question. Maybe that's how they got those heavy bars in.'

Ralph studied him. 'Heavy bars?'

'Don't you remember me telling you I paid two gold bars for the encyclopaedias over there.' He pointed to the set of Brittanica's.

'You didn't say anything about any gold.'

Mad Bill scratched his head. 'Come to think of it, I probably didn't. If I told you all my secrets as soon as you got here, we'd soon run out of things to talk about, and we're going to have each other's company for a long, long time, unless, of course, I die soon.'

Ralph glared at him. 'There must be some way for me to get off this island?'

'Hardly anyone comes here nowadays, more's the pity. Where's the bloke selling gym equipment when you need him?'

Ralph looked at him blankly. 'Don't you think you've left your run a bit late to start working out.'

'Not me, sonny. You! You're not fooling me dressed in that get-up. You don't look strong enough to carry me all the way to the cemetery?'

Ralph's nostrils flared. 'You don't get it, do you? You might want to die here but I won't rest until I work out a way to go home.'

'Please yourself. It's your breath you're wasting. But if I was you I wouldn't be fighting it. You're probably never going to get off this island. My advice to you, sonny, is to relax.'

'Will you stop calling me sonny.'

'I call everyone younger than me sonny. That way I can't get their name mixed up.'

'But I'm the only one here. You're not likely to mix me up with someone else!'

'Suppose not, what did you say your name was? Whatever it is, you're welcome to share my gold now that you're here. But a fat lot of good it will do you. You can only buy so many encyclopaedias, assuming that salesman ever comes here again.'

Ralph buried his face in his hands. When he glanced up, he said: 'If you actually have all this gold, and I'm not saying you do, why didn't you buy the computer and satellite dish?'

'Do you think I came down in the last shower?' The pitch of his voice rose and dropped like a rollercoaster. 'You just can't send stuff through the air. You need wires.'

Ralph waved his hands. 'You would have been able to send an email for help.'

He looked at Ralph as if he were stupid. 'Email? Isn't that a brand of fridge?'

'I don't believe it! You stood for the Senate, and you don't know what email is? How were you planning to communicate with your constituents?'

'The old-fashioned way! Door-knocking!'

'And how were you planning to get to the mainland to do this door-knocking?'

'I wasn't. If they really wanted to know something, they'd have to come out here and knock on *my* door.'

'And you planned to answer?'

'Only armed with my shotgun. You can't be too careful. I remember a day when a white man could control his own land. Look at it now? People don't have respect for the flag any more. Anyone would think we didn't actually win the war! And don't talk to me about the Chinese and them Arabs.'

'Let me guess: you were standing for the looney right?'

Mad Bill waggled a finger angrily. 'You'll thank me one day.'

'But you didn't actually get in!'

'We'll no, not as far as I know. I first stood many years ago in Hobart but I had to do a runner before the polls were declared, which means I never knew if I had won or not. I got the political itch again years later, but I don't know how that went either. As I said, the mailman used to come by every few months. He delivered my letter to a political party in Canberra, which wrote back and said they'd be delighted to have me as their Senate candidate because my views perfectly aligned with theirs.' He shook his head. 'Never did find out what happened to that postie. Darkey just stopped coming.'

'Darkey? Not the same Darkey I met on the boat? About 6 foot 2, built like a brick shithouse, bald ...'

'Sounds like the same bloke. Do you know what became of him?'

'He went to jail, as far as I can gather.'

'Jail?' Mad Bill got up and walked over to the drinks cabinet, which was made from walnut with lead-light glass. He poured the sherry. 'Lovely drop, this.' He sighed as he handed Ralph his glass. 'I've always prided myself on being a good judge of character. Darkey seemed like such a fine upstanding chap. He wouldn't even take any money from me.'

Mad Bill returned to his chair and sat down. 'If he went to jail that would explain why I never heard back about the election date.'

'How were you planning to vote?'

'I wasn't. I was going to exercise my democratic right not to vote.'

'I think you'll find voting is compulsory in Australia.'

'Well, that was one of my platforms. If I got into the Senate, I was going to lobby against compulsory voting. It's been one of the ruinations of our democracy. The do-gooders keep getting in.'

They were on their fourth glass of sherry when they heard knocking on the front door. It wasn't just one or two polite knocks. It sounded like someone trying to batter the door down.

Mad Bill reached into his pocket and pulled out a fob watch on a golden chain. He opened the lid and examined it. 'He's back already! At this time of night?'

'Who's back?'

'It could only be the real estate agent. But I didn't hear his boat, did you?'

'I thought you said he was only here last week?'

'You know how persistent real estate agents can be.'

'We should answer it. It might be my ticket off the island.'

'Nooooo.'

Mad Bill was too slow. Ralph was already headed for the passage, which was illuminated by a candle hanging from the wall as if Mad Bill *was* expecting someone to visit.

Ralph dragged the door open, and found Hendrik looking down at him. The skipper was dripping and was holding a buoyancy ring.

NINETEEN
DAVY DIDN'T MAKE IT

'SO, YOU *ARE* HERE?' Hendrik slumped forward.

Ralph broke his fall and was enveloped in a wet embrace. 'More to the point, how did *you* get here?'

'It took me hours to swim.' Hendrik buried his head in Ralph's shoulder. 'Can I come in? I really need to sit down.'

Mad Bill, who was hovering behind them, sighed. 'I suppose so. Whack him down on the plastic chair.' He waggled a finger at Hendrik. 'But I'm a wake-up to you, sonny! If you thought you could just waltz in here barefoot and get my good furniture all wet …'

He didn't finish his sentence. Instead, he prised the buoyancy ring from Hendrik's hand. 'That's not coming in though! I can see it's got sand on it.' He threw the buoyancy ring down next to the shotgun near the entrance as Ralph helped Hendrik inside and into the chair.

'Thank you,' Hendrik said. 'I thought I was a goner.'

Mad Bill disappeared from the room and returned with a towel he handed to Hendrik. Hendrik's emotions unleashed in a cascade of tears.

'Sorry.' He tried to hide his head in his hands.

Ralph bent down and wrapped his arm around the skipper's shoulders. 'It's all right.'

Hendrik looked sideways at Ralph. 'But it's not all right. Don't you understand? Davy is dead.'

As the stinky candles on the sideboard flickered, Hendrik explained how he had emerged from the cabin after his sleep and wondered where everyone was. First, he had checked out the galley. No-one was there, and there was no evidence anyone had been there recently. No cooking smells, no dirty pans. So he had gone to the wheelhouse to ask Davy where everyone was, and that's where he had seen Whitey and Darkey. As he approached, Whitey had raised a gun to his head.

'I should never have brought them both aboard.'

'Darkey didn't have a gun then?' Mad Bill said.

Hendrik looked up, his cheeks awash with tears. 'Know him, do you?'

'He used to be my mailboat man.'

'I presume you're Senator Mad Bill?'

'Don't call me Senator.' The old man's voice became shrill and his eyes became wild.

'Darkey didn't have a gun. But he didn't stop Whitey either. Next thing I knew someone had pushed me overboard. When I came up for air I heard splashing. It was Davy spitting water and panicking as he tried not to go under. They had thrown him overboard just before me.'

'How did they expect to drive the boat without you both?' Ralph said.

Hendrik pinched his eyebrows. 'Darkey knows what to do, on the open water at least. I don't know how he'll go parking it. Though if he used to operate the mailboat, maybe he knows more than I give him credit for.'

'So what happened to Davy?' Ralph stood and crossed to another chair.

Hendrik's face contorted again. 'I knew he was thick but the dumbo never told me he couldn't swim! What kind of deckhand can't swim? I would have made him wear a life vest on the boat.'

He hung his head. 'He starts screaming: "Help, I can't swim." Next thing, someone throws a buoyancy ring from the boat. Who does that? It just gave him false hope that he'd be all right.'

'Darkey threw it?' Ralph knew he was the more compassionate of the two hoods.

'Maybe, but I reckon it was Whitey. I bet he was the kind of kid who removed the wings from flies just to see them suffer.'

'And you didn't pick up on that the night you drugged him and Darkey in the pub?'

'There were warning signs but I just didn't join the dots until I was in the water and had a lot of time to think about it. I had just assumed that Darkey, being much older, would call the shots. I mean, Whitey just looks like a long and lanky long-haired kid!'

His eyes welled up again.

'Davy didn't deserve to die like that. I could accept it if we had been wrecked by a storm. I mean, that's an occupational hazard. But the sea was so calm today.' He banged his hand on the arm of the chair.

'You saw him go under, sonny?'

Hendrik looked up at Mad Bill, then to Ralph.

'You being here is really going to do his head in,' Ralph advised Hendrik. 'Just go with *sonny* for the time being.'

'It was light when we started out,' Hendrik said. 'The trawler just pulled away and left us treading water. I swam over to Davy and grabbed the other side of his buoyancy ring. He wanted to know what we were going to do now. But what could we do? No-one was likely to rescue us. We had to swim to safety. He kept saying he didn't want to die. I told him, nobody was going to die, but it might be helpful if I knew where I was so I knew which way to swim. That's when he told me they had left you at Senator Mad Bill's Island about an hour before.'

'I've already warned you.' Mad Bill waggled a finger again.

'Warned me of what?'

'I'm not a bloody senator.'

Hendrik just stared, and then said: 'It might have only taken the boat an hour to come that distance, but it took a lot longer on a rubber ring. When the daylight faded and we still hadn't sighted the island, I thought we were both goners. Then it got dark. Overcast, too. You couldn't even see the moon.'

'But Davy was still with you?'

'Well, he was. But then he wasn't. I realised after a while I was talking to myself, and he must have let go. Poor bugger must have been so tired.'

'But you don't know for sure he drowned?' Ralph said.

'I told you: he couldn't swim. He had no chance without the buoyancy ring.'

TWENTY
NO ONE'S GETTING OFF THIS ISLAND

HENDRIK SAID he had almost given up, too, until he saw the flickering lights of the island. Those dim lights gave him new hope to start paddling again.

It took him at least another hour to get here. It might have been longer, it was hard to tell. Every time he thought he was close enough in to just about touch the bottom, the current pulled him back out a little again.

Mad Bill blew out a whoosh of air. 'Guess this means I have to make up another bed?'

'Is that a problem?' Ralph said.

'I have plenty of rooms, sonny. It's the linen and blankets I might have trouble with.'

'It'll only be for a night or two.' Hendrik suddenly brightened and he held up a bit of the towel. 'If I can just get a few hours' sleep, I'll nut out just how we can get home.'

Mad Bill made a raspberry noise. 'You blokes don't get it, do you? None of youse are getting off this island.'

He turned his attention to Ralph. 'This must make you happier. Now you might have someone to bury you.'

TWENTY-ONE
HE'S GOTTA BE FISH FOOD BY NOW

MAD BILL SAID he couldn't be sure if the bunks had been left by the British army.

'The people who ran the leper colony might have left them here,' he said as he led them up the wide, carpeted stairs.

Ralph stopped with such abruptness the breeze his flapping shirt created nearly blew out the single candle he was carrying on a small brass tray, which had a little grip ring at the end. Hendrik nearly crashed into the back of him. Mad Bill kept charging on but turned at the top of the landing when he sensed no-one was behind him.

'Why have you stopped?' Mad Bill had a candle in one hand and gripped the rail with the other.

'Did you say *leper* colony?' Ralph looked up at him.

'I did, didn't I?' He cackled. 'But I don't know that for sure. The island might have been used to quarantine people with some other type of infectious disease. All I know for sure is at least some of them died here. Whether they left the bunks and the pile of grey blankets in the cupboard, we'll never know.'

Ralph stepped up six or seven steps so he could look Mad Bill in the eye. 'I hope you've washed the blankets in boiling water?'

The old man held Ralph's gaze. 'Where would I get boiling water from? What's the big deal, anyway, sonny? Everyone has to die. You only need to outlast me by a day or two.'

Ralph was still shaking his head when Mad Bill showed them to their room first on the left at the top of the landing.

They chose the two bottom bunks, and Hendrik fell asleep as soon as his head hit the pillow. Poor bloke was exhausted. He had probably never counted on a sleep he was going to wake up from.

Something caught Ralph's eye as he was about to blow out the smelly candle and get into bed. Something was carved into the wooden bedhead of his bunk.

He brought the candle closer. Ahhhh. He screwed up his nose as the acrid stench became even more offensive. The carving said 'B.Y. was here'. Someone else had carved in a different hand beneath it, 'And died here.'

Oh great. This was becoming a habit, sleeping in beds where dead people had been. Ralph relocated his bedding to the top bunk. That done, he blew out the candle and climbed the ladder.

As Hendrik started to snore gently, Ralph lay there thinking.

It had been his second exhausting day in a row. He wondered what Maria was doing right now?

She was probably not sleeping either, believing she was a heavily pregnant grieving widow.

Assuming no-one had seen him being picked up by the fishing boat, everyone would think he was dead. Drowned. Like poor Davy. Hendrik was right. He hadn't deserved to die like that. Did Whitey and Darkey really think they were going to get away with this?

But they would get away with it, wouldn't they?

The authorities would never find Davy's body out here.

And what were the odds of Hendrik and him ever being rescued? Even if Mad Bill was wrong about them never getting off this island, the way his luck was running he'd be busy at the tree the one time the real estate agent arrived. He obviously couldn't trust the old man to come get him. The old man might be willing to part with one potential pall-bearer, but not both of them.

Hendrik let out a long groan in his sleep. Ralph looked over the side, but it was too dark to see. He imagined him tugging at his hair. Poor sod. It must have been a traumatic moment, looking up to see Davy was gone.

Davy wouldn't have had time on the boat to get off a mayday message either, so no-one would be looking for them.

Nor would they be looking for Ralph.

His daughter would grow up without a father now.

Or worse, with someone else she called dad. Ralph bit his lip and he could feel his tears welling up.

He couldn't blame Maria if she wanted to take the baby back to Lisbon. It wasn't just the issue of securing permanent residency without him, she'd probably want to be close to her own family support base. Her mother, her sisters. And as hard as it was to think about it, Ralph knew another man would come into her life. How could he blame anyone? Maria was a beautiful young woman. It would be selfish of him to wish she'd spend the rest of her life alone.

It was cold and Ralph felt he had no choice but to pull up the dubious blanket over his shoulders. He rolled over and sobbed into his equally dubious pillow, which he punched again and again.

TWENTY-TWO
RUBBER DUCKIES TO THE RESCUE

RALPH HAD no idea what time it was awakened.

Even if he had been able to see in the dark, he knew his watch had immortalised the time the angry mob had chased him into the bay.

He assumed at first his bladder had woken him up.

Well, it figured. Ralph shouldn't have had that last sherry. That was the trouble with 80-year-old fortified wine. It was too darn nice to turn down. Why couldn't Mad Bill have given them a piss pot too? Now he'd have to find his way downstairs in the dark and find a small tree near to the house. No way was he running the gauntlet of rats to get to the big tree!

Hendrik was still snoring down below.

Ralph didn't feel as sorry for him now. He had probably peed into the ocean. That was probably the only good thing about being set adrift. You could go when you wanted, and no-one would know.

Hendrik hadn't drunk any of the sherry either.

Ralph wondered how long it'd actually be before daylight came through the window.

Perhaps he had much longer than a couple of hours to wait? He had no idea how much sleep he had actually had.

He touched his cheeks, and found no signs of wetness. That probably meant he had been asleep for at least an hour.

His thoughts were disturbed by knocking downstairs.

He held his breath and listened.

Someone was knocking on the front door.

It turned into pounding, then distant yelling.

It wasn't easy finding the ladder in the dark, and scrambling down it.

He expected Hendrik to wake up any second with all the noise. But he kept snoring.

He felt his way across the room and as soon as he opened the door he saw Mad Bill coming down the stairs. He was carrying a lighted candle in one hand and his false teeth in the other, and he was wearing a Rip Van Winkle sleep hat.

Ralph felt suddenly under-dressed because he was just wearing his boxer shorts.

But Mad Bill didn't seem to notice.

It was hard to understand him without his false teeth in, but Ralph managed to decipher it. 'I told you that real estate man was coming back tonight,' he said gummily. 'These people just won't take no for an answer.'

Ralph led the way down the dimly lit stairs.

He opened the door, and saw immediately Mad Bill had jumped to the wrong conclusion.

Two muscular, heavily tattooed arms fell into him. Davy! On the step behind him were two of the biggest yellow rubber ducks Ralph had ever seen.

'I'm so, so sorry,' Davy sobbed. 'I saw Hendrik drown.'

TWENTY-THREE
BUT I SAW HIM DROWN

RALPH HELPED DAVY inside and sat him down on the plastic chair. Good thing Hendrik's towel was still there because Mad Bill draped it over Davy's shoulders.

Davy was shivering, his teeth were chattering and his bare feet were blue.

'Do you have a heater?' Ralph turned to Mad Bill, who was standing behind him.

'I already told you, sonny. I've only got a wood fire, and I can only get to the wood at low tide. But I'll get another warm towel you can wrap around him. There's a cupboard full of them in the kitchen.'

Ralph put both hands on Davy's shoulders.

'Listen to me. Hendrik is not dead.'

Davy tossed his head from side to side. 'But I saw him go down.'

'Delirium will make you see things. You've been in the water a long time.'

Davy stopped tossing his head and squinted at Ralph. 'Do I know you?'

'You rescued me from the bay, remember?'

'You look different.'

Ralph became conscious he was standing in front of him wearing only his boxers. It's a good thing Mad Bill re-entered the room. His smile told Ralph he was wearing his false teeth again, and he was actually carrying two towels. 'Thanks,' Ralph said, as he gave Davy a second layer and covered his own shoulders with the other one.

'My ducks,' mumbled Davy. 'Where are my ducks?'

Mad Bill looked at Ralph.

'I'll go get them.'

Ralph went outside. It took him a few minutes because he seized the opportunity to fertilise a shrub, but when he returned he was carrying one duck in each hand.

Davy was sipping on a glass of sherry, and had stopped shivering.

'Where did *they* come from?' Mad Bill said when he laid eyes on the oversized yellow bath-toys. 'Are they what I think they are?'

'They saved my life,' Davy said. 'One minute I was holding on to the ring with Hendrik, the next minute it was gone and so was he.'

'I thought you said you saw him drown?' Ralph said.

'That was later, and he was a long way away.'

'But Hendrik said it was so dark, he couldn't see anything out there.'

Davy took another sip.

'Well, it was, and it wasn't. It was black as black when I realised I was no longer hanging on to the ring, I thought, well, this was it. I laid back in the water and waited to sink. And waited. And waited. After a few minutes, I realised I was still breathing air. Then I realised I was actually floating on my back. First time in my life I've ever floated. I guess I just relaxed.'

'You picked a good time to discover that skill.' Ralph smiled.

'What happened next was even better than that. For a couple of minutes, the clouds parted and the moon shone down into my eyes. It was almost blinding, and the light made me turn my head. It's then I saw I was in the middle of a flotilla of dozens of rubber ducks.'

'So you grabbed hold of these two?' Ralph said.

He nodded, and drained his glass.

Mad Bill stamped his foot like he was about to start a jig. 'I *knew* I had seen those ducks before.' He walked over to the cabinet and got the sherry bottle. 'They look smaller out on the water though.'

'What are the odds of two lots of rubber ducks falling off container ships?' Ralph said.

Mad Bill filled Davy's glass again. 'Beats me. I just can't get over the size of those things. Who'd give a child something that big to play with in the bath? They'd be scared to death.'

Davy seemed to like what he was now tossing back. 'Well, these ducks saved my life. I doubt I could have made it all this way without their extra buoyancy.'

'So what made you think Hendrik drowned?'

'I could have sworn I saw him go under, just before the clouds hid the moon again. Mind you, he was 20 or 30 yards away from me.'

TWENTY-FOUR
GLOW OF THE DEAD

MAD BILL CAME DOWN to the bottom of the steps and handed them a grey blanket and another malodorous candle. 'I can't help you with more linen though.' His Rip Van Winkle shook as he spoke. 'Who knew I'd ever get this many visitors!'

Davy seemed to be fully hydrated again and over his shakes. He had towelled himself dry. He didn't want to leave his ducks but Ralph had persuaded him they would be fine in the lounge room for the rest of the night.

Davy took the steps two at a time as he bounded into the gloom.

He was waiting at the bedroom door for Ralph.

'Here, take this.' Davy screwed up his face when Ralph handed him the candle so he could open the door.

The smell wiped the smile off his face but it was nothing compared with the look on Hendrik's face when he saw the ghostly face of a man he thought to be dead coming through the door.

Hendrik raised a finger, uttered something incoherent and collapsed unconscious back on to his pillow.

TWENTY-FIVE
COOKING CANDLES

RALPH AWOKE several hours later to light coming through the window and an awful smell wafting up from downstairs. Two different lots of snoring were coming from the bunks below.

He climbed down the ladder as stealthily as he could. Hendrik and Davy deserved to sleep all day after their ordeal. He only hoped when Hendrik did wake up he'd realise Davy wasn't actually a ghost.

Ralph dressed and went downstairs, where he found Mad Bill stirring a pot on a wood stove in the kitchen.

'What are you cooking?' Ralph screwed up his nose.

'Candles.'

'Candles?'

'Not to eat. Though I suppose you could eat the tallow if you were hungry enough.'

Ralph looked over his shoulder, and the source of the smell became apparent. He was boiling a rat, and this one did have fur and whiskers, but no eyeballs left to speak of, and the fat was bubbling to the surface.

Mad Bill took one look at Ralph's face and said: 'You'll get used to it, sonny.' He was dressed again in the same checked blue shirt and brown suspenders. 'I normally only have to do this about once a month. But we're going to need a lot more candles now there are four of us on this island.'

'I think I'd rather stumble around in the dark.'

'No, you wouldn't. You wouldn't want to trip over a rat in your bedroom.'

'They're in the house!'

'Well, below the house mainly. Lots of them live in the tunnels. I only ever go down into the basement for one of five things. A bottle of sherry. Paint. More ammo; there are boxes and boxes down there. A gold bar. Or a rat for the pot.'

'How many rats live in these tunnels?'

The old man shrugged. 'Thousands? Hundreds of thousands? Too many to count, that's for sure.'

Ralph looked over at the pot again. Even a dead and cooking rat seemed threatening to him.

'You're not scared of them?'

Mad Bill scratched his head. 'Why would I be scared of them? I'm way ahead on the kill count.'

'I didn't hear the shotgun go off this morning?'

Mad Bill laughed. 'Oh no, you wouldn't want to fire a gun down there. Too many stone walls for the pellets to ricochet off. No, I just wait at the entrance of the tunnel and knock them on the head with a piece of wood.'

He walked to the other side of the kitchen and opened a cupboard. 'Do you want some of these for your breakfast? Or should I heat up a bit of that stew you really liked.'

TWENTY-SIX
LAST WILL AND TESTAMENT

THE CUPBOARD WAS full of boxes of breakfast cereal. 'Where did that all come from?' Ralph gasped.

'Didn't I tell you about the breakfast-food salesman who came to the island?'

Mad Bill opened another cupboard which was stacked with cartons of long-life milk. 'I had to pay one gold ingot for the cereal, and another for the milk. He said he could get me a cow but that would cost more. I told him not to bother because I wasn't about to give him any more of my gold.'

'As if he could get a cow to the island anyway!' Ralph said.

'Nothing would surprise me.' Mad Bill chuckled. 'The first time the real estate man came he was flying an ultralight plane. He hadn't even planned to land here, he dropped out of the sun like Icarus. I told him the island wasn't for sale, and that he was lucky he hadn't got shotgun pellets in his undercarriage, but he just wouldn't take no for an answer. Same with the cow bloke! He insisted he'd come back but I told him if he does he better come armed.'

Mad Bill sighed. Or it could have been a wheeze. 'Anyway, I suppose there's one good thing about you three being here now.'

He picked up an envelope from the counter and handed it over.

'What's this?' Ralph stared at the sealed envelope.

'Don't open it till I'm gone.'

Ralph glared at him, hoping the silence would draw more information from him.

'If you must know, it's outlining the music I want for my funeral.'

'Music! Where do you think we'll get that from?' He lowered his voice and looked around. 'Don't tell me you're bought a whole lot of MP3 players?'

'A whole lot of what?'

'They're devices for playing digital music.'

Mad Bill laughed. 'No, the gold bars are nearly all spent.'

'You're skint?'

'Not quite. I still have two more pallets in the cellar.' He pointed to the floor. 'I pity the three of you having to bring it all up to the graveyard.'

'What?'

He stepped towards Ralph and stabbed at the envelope. 'It's all in there. I want to be buried with all the gold. Like a pharaoh.'

'I thought you said this was all about the music you wanted?'

'That too. I thought you blokes could sing three-part harmonies.'

TWENTY-SEVEN
CAN YOU POINT THE WAY?

RALPH COULDN'T FACE either variety of breakfast, so he left Mad Bill to his candle-making and went off to explore the island, careful to avoid anywhere he suspected snakes might be lying in wait.

He had to go through the graveyard again, then returned to the house via the other side of the island, where he got a glimpse of the wrecks of the old ships poking out in the water and the veggie plot by the side of the house. Corn, lettuce, tomatoes, zucchinis, marrows, peas and beans were thriving. He wondered how many gold bars Mad Bill had paid for those seeds?

Next to the garden was a well, with a bucket on a rope, and he drew some water, which he cupped in his hands to drink. Then he sat on a low wall for a while and tried to think what he was going to do.

Ralph was just going in through the front door when he saw Hendrik and Davy coming downstairs side by side and laughing. 'You're still a dumb-fuck,' he heard the skipper say.

Ralph looked up. 'I thought you two would probably sleep all day after what you went through.'

'*Au contraire,*' the skipper said. 'It's good to be alive. We're ready for the next *aventure.*'

Ralph had never heard him speaking French before. Actually, he remembered he had. He had mentioned the *au natural* toilet on the fishing boat.

By now they had reached the bottom of the stairs. Hendrik put his arm around Ralph and whispered. 'We actually both need to use the *toilette*. Can you point the way?'

Ralph looked down at Hendrik's gnarly toenails. 'What happened to your shoes?'

'We kicked our rubber boots off when we went into the water, along with the bib and braces. Otherwise we'd have drowned.'

Ralph was thankful now he hadn't even had time to think about jettisoning his black running shoes in the water.

'You'll have to be careful not to tread on a snake then,' Ralph said.

Hendrik looked at him with a puzzled look. 'Is it an outside loo?'

'Yep. It's on the other side of the island, just past the cemetery.'

'The what?'

'Follow me.' Ralph turned around. 'I'll explain on the way.'

Ralph made a diversion to the kitchen to tell Mad Bill where they were going. The awful smell was still there, but the pot was gone and so was the old man.

'Hello,' he called, but there was no answer.

Hendrik frowned. 'Where's he gone?'

'I have no idea. He couldn't have gone far. Maybe he's down by the tunnels?'

'This place has tunnels?' Hendrik had the look of a man who's just realised he'd won the lottery. 'Do they go to the mainland?'

Ralph shrugged, and headed towards the door. 'We'll talk on the way. Mind where you step.'

TWENTY-EIGHT

THE THREE PALLBEARERS

THEY SAT down on the park bench at the graveyard and Ralph filled them in. He told them about the tunnels and the ammo and the sherry and the rats and the snakes but it was the mention of the gold that really got their attention.

'Do senators really earn that much?' Davy said.

The other two looked around at him.

'He's not really a senator,' Ralph said.

'Well, why's he called Senator Mad Bill then?'

'Didn't you listen to Darkey? It's a joke. But the thing is, the joke is on everyone else. As far as I can tell, he doesn't pay taxes and he only has to put up with a few island-hopping salesmen.'

Hendrik frowned. 'Who he pays in gold bars?'

'Or so he says. My theory is that it's a figment of his imagination.'

'What if it isn't?' Hendrik said. 'What if he's on the level? Do you think he'll want to share that gold? To keep his secret?'

Ralph pointed to a patch of ground in front of him. 'I doubt it. I think he thinks it might come in handy in the afterlife. He wants to be buried with it.'

Hendrik looked down at the unused plot. 'Here?'

'Yep, right here. And he wants us to sing at his funeral.'

'Sing?' Hendrik looked from face to face. 'My wife doesn't even let me sing in the shower.'

'I don't think he cares,' Ralph said. 'Yesterday, he was resigned to just curling up and dying, and letting the rats feed on him. Now he's found three pall-bearers.'

'The Three Singing Pall-bearers,' Davy said, bursting into a grin. 'Can I be Pavarotti?'

Hendrik stared at him until the smile disappeared. 'You do know he's the fat dead one?'

Hendrik rubbed his stubbled chin. 'This is another good reason to get off this island as soon as we can.' He looked from face to face again. 'Any ideas?'

'If we can just get your fishing boat back again …?' Davy's voice trailed off.

Hendrik sighed. 'Fingers crossed, we'll never see that rust bucket again.'

'How can you say that?' Davy looked pained. 'That was our livelihood.'

'No, it was just my way to get out of the house for six weeks,' Hendrik said. 'Truth is the bottom has fallen out of the fishing business. Catches have fallen, quotas have tightened. The good thing is the insurance is worth more than what that trawler is even worth now.'

He stood up. 'Now if you don't mind, I really need that toilet.'

Davy got up too, but Hendrik said: 'You'll have to wait your turn, Pavarotti.'

When they looked towards the big tree, a horrible sight came into focus.

Mad Bill was sitting on a branch over the water. So that's where he had gone?

Seeing his trousers down to his ankles was bad enough, but there was even a more disturbing sight behind him.

They could see a yellow life-raft rapidly approaching the island.

'Be buggered!' Hendrik said. 'That's from *The Good Lady*!'

TWENTY-NINE
MY GUN IS BIGGER THAN YOUR GUN

'WHAT ARE WE GOING TO DO?' Davy's eyes widened.

'What *can* we do?' Ralph said. 'They're coming this way and we know Whitey has a gun.'

Hendrik slapped his thigh. 'Didn't I see a shotgun lying against the wall near the front door of the house?' He squinted towards the life-raft as if he were trying to calculate how long it was going to take them to reach the island.

Ralph braved another look at Mad Bill. He was in his own little world. He hadn't even appeared to notice the three men coming out of the graveyard, let alone the yellow raft coming this way with at least one more visitor, maybe two.

Ralph shook his head. 'We can't go shooting people with Mad Bill's gun!'

'I just want to scare them, maybe splash them with a few rounds. Make them change course to another island.'

'I dunno. Maybe we should check with Mad Bill. Perhaps he should do the shooting? It's his shotgun.'

'You're kidding me?' Hendrik pointed a finger. 'Look at him! How long do you think it will take him to get his pants up and get back to the house.'

He raised his finger a bit higher. 'And how long do you think it'll take them to get to the island?'

He had a good point. They turned for the house.

THIRTY

WHERE'D THEY GO?

HENDRIK PICKED up the shotgun and raised it to his eye. 'This feels good for an antique. Those boys won't know what hit them.'

'You said you *wouldn't* hit them?' Ralph said.

'Relax, will you? No-one's about to shoot anyone. But believe me, blokes like Whitey only understand one thing. When I fire a few shots off and he gets the message my gun is bigger than his gun, he'll think twice about coming closer.'

He started running towards the other side of the island, with the two of them right behind. How could he go so fast in bare feet?

They kept running through the cemetery towards the tree, where they found Mad Bill back on the ground buttoning up his trousers.

'Hey, what are you doing with my gun, sonny?' he croaked when he looked up.

'Protecting you, that's what,' Hendrik said. 'I never thought I'd be thanking a crazy old man for keeping a loaded shotgun leaning against his hallway wall.'

'I'm not crazy. I'm mad; there's a difference.'

Hendrik thumbed towards the ocean. 'I can't believe you didn't see them coming.' Then a puzzled look came over him as he realised the raft wasn't there any more. 'Where'd they go?'

'Where'd who go?' Mad Bill turned and looked at the waves rolling towards the shore. A seabird dive-bombed for fish, but that was the only other thing going on.

Hendrik looked from Davy to Ralph. 'You blokes saw it, tell him.' They nodded.

'It doesn't matter none,' Mad Bill said. 'Did you really think that gun was loaded?'

Hendrik went white. Ralph could swear he had a plughole in his neck and someone had let all the blood from his face go down the drain. He cracked the shotgun open, looked inside, and turned even a whiter shade of pale.

Then Mad Bill went all white too, like he had seen a ghost.

None of the others had time to turn around.

When he heard the click, Ralph half-turned and saw there was a hand gun right up against the back of Hendrik's head.

The skipper dropped the shotgun at the very moment Ralph felt a sharp jab on the side of his neck.

Someone sniffed. Ralph didn't have to do a lot of guessing to work out who that was.

'I knew we should have just killed the three of you,' Whitey said. 'I know how the journalist boy got here — against my better judgement, as it happens. But you two blokes? How the hell did you get here? I would have put someone else's money on you being squeezed out through the arse end of a shark by now.'

He sniffed again. 'Speaking of which, what's that smell?'

THIRTY-ONE

BEST MAILMAN I EVER HAD

'CHRIST, IT smells even worse in here than over there,' Whitey said after they had marched their captives back to the house and into the lounge.

'You'll get used to it, sonny.' Mad Bill still had his hands up like the others. He looked at the man armed with the spanner that had been pressed to Ralph's neck. 'Tell him Darkey.'

Darkey looked at his shoes.

Whitey sniffed. 'You didn't tell me you actually know this old fart?'

'I tried to tell you in the raft but I couldn't find the right moment. Back when I was trying to go straight, this island was one of the stopping points on my mailboat route.'

'Best mailman I ever had too.' Then Mad Bill said in a softer voice: 'Only mailman I've had, come to think of it.'

Whitey tapped his forehead with his gun. 'Will you shut up, old man. I need to think, and that smell isn't making it any easier. What the fuck is it?'

'I've been making candles. Now you two are here, I'm going to have to make a whole lot more.'

Whitey sniffed.

'He boils the rats down for tallow in the kitchen.' Ralph said. 'It's probably a good use of the resources he has on hand. This island is infested with rats. Apparently, they're worst of all down in the cellar.'

'Oh, that's gross.' Whitey turned to Darkey. 'I thought back on the boat you were joking about the rats to put the wind up journalist boy here. You know how much I hate rats! Why did you even bring me here?'

'It's not like we had a lot of choice.'

'You said you knew how to drive that fishing boat?'

Darkey shrugged. 'I didn't count on being shirt-fronted by a partly submerged shipping container. Besides, how was I to know you were freaked out by rats? I always thought it was snakes.'

Whitey banged the gun again against his forehead, which was beaded up with sweat. When he reopened his eyes, he sniffed. 'Can't you turn the extractor fan on, old man. It really stinks in here.'

'Well, you're not making the air any sweeter, sonny.'

Whitey pointed the gun at him. 'You better be more careful what you are saying.'

Mad Bill stuck out his chin. 'Think I'm scared of you? What's the worse you can do? Kill me? Do you really think that worries me at my age?'

Whitey laughed. 'Depends how I decide to kill you. What if I do you slowly? Tell you what? You go and fix us some grub, and I'll put my mind to it.'

Mad Bill scampered to the kitchen but Whitey called him back. He prodded the old man's chest with his index finger. 'And no funny business, old man. If I look down at my plate and see rat, the rest of your life won't be worth living. That's. A. Promise.'

THIRTY-TWO
NO, NO, NOT THAT

WHITEY DIDN'T WAIT LONG before deciding what to do with Mad Bill and the three others.

The cogs of his macabre mind must have started turning as soon as Mad Bill had left the room.

'I wish the boys in H Block could see me now. I've just had a brainwave.'

'Another one?' Darkey said. 'What do you have in mind this time?'

Whitey sniffed his brains back in again. He waved the gun from Ralph to Davy and then to Hendrik. 'Can you boys guess what I have in store for you?'

Davy said: 'You're going to let us go?'

Ralph didn't think he meant it seriously, more as a joke to break the ice. But Hendrik had to take it one step further, didn't he? 'Don't make him angry, you dumb fruitcake,' he mumbled.

'What did you just call me?' Whitey's dark look became darker.

'Not you! Him!' Hendrik pointed to Davy. 'But he's just Dumb. You two are Dumber and Dumbest.'

Next thing, the skipper went down like a sack of potatoes. He was on the floor with blood streaming down his head, where Whitey had just pistol-whipped him.

Whitey snarled: 'You're going to regret opening your mouth, captain, when the rats smell that blood.'

Whitey broke into laughter. 'See, if you had just listened a moment instead of being a comedian, I would have told you about what I have in store.'

He put a hand on Ralph's shoulder. 'No need to thank me. Thank your clever reporter friend.'

Ralph felt eyes locking on him from all directions.

'He's the one who told me there are rats in the cellar, and I think it'll do you all some good if we lock you in there for a while.' Whitey flashed his yellow teeth. 'That OK with you boys?'

At that moment, Mad Bill returned from the kitchen. 'I've left two bowls on the table in there. You're just lucky we had leftovers from last night.'

'And it's your lucky day too, old man.' Whitey pointed the gun. 'Lead the way to the cellar.'

Fear flashed into the old man's eyes. 'Please, not that. Not the rat-infested cellar. Shoot me now. Please.'

Whitey sniffed. 'Oh, no. You don't get out of this life that easily. Go on, lead the way.'

Mad Bill headed to a door off the lounge that led to a long narrow stone stairwell.

Davy and Ralph helped Hendrik across the room to the top of the stairs but there was no space to flank him going down, and he just had to do the best he could himself.

Whitey and Darkey brought up the rear, but Whitey stopped halfway down and flattened himself against the wall so Darkey could squeeze past. 'I'm not going any further. Just make sure you lock the door after them.'

Darkey obviously didn't care for rats either.

He pushed their captives inside as quickly as he could and slammed the big metal door shut. Ralph heard the lock turn and bolts slide.

THIRTY-THREE
SCREAMS FROM ABOVE

MAD BILL DISAPPEARED into the dark, they heard a match being struck and suddenly there was flickering light.

So he kept the stinky candles on the wall down here too?

As Mad Bill stepped away from the ledge, Ralph looked around at their prison.

The walls were reinforced with some kind of brickwork.

Some odd tools hung on one of the walls.

Inside one of the tunnel openings he could see boxes, lots of paint tins and packing cases stacked on top of each other. Out the front of the entrance was one of those big Mary Poppins prams covered in cobwebs. So they used to have infectious babies here too?

'Where are the rats?' Ralph said. 'I thought there'd be lots of rats.'

Mad Bill laughed. 'Did you like my great acting? I'm waiting for an Academy Award nomination. I tell people that story so they're too scared to come down here and steal my sherry and gold.'

'You really do have gold then?' Ralph looked around. 'Where is it?'

Mad Bill pointed to the tunnel on the right.' In there. You can't see it because the bars are stacked on pallets.'

'But no rats?'

'I imagine there are plenty of them deep in the tunnel, but not here. They never come out here. The smell of the candles keeps them away.'

Ralph coughed. 'Yes, it is a bit acrid, isn't it?'

'You'll get used to it, sonny.' He pointed to the left-hand tunnel. 'There's all kind of stuff in those boxes over there.'

It was about now they heard the scream from upstairs. Funny, Ralph hadn't expected to hear anything through these thick walls.

He could only assume it was a very loud scream.

He had wondered how far into his meal Whitey would get before he realised he was eating snake?

THIRTY-FOUR
GOOD THINGS HAPPEN IN THE DARK

HENDRIK FORGOT HIS PAIN. 'I can't believe they were so stupid to lock us down here without checking it out first. They'd have no idea there are two escape tunnels down here.'

But Mad Bill urged caution. 'I have no idea where they go.'

'Who cares where they go,' Hendrik said. 'Imagine the look on Darkey's and Whitey's faces when they check on us in the morning and find there's no bugger here.'

'Well, I'll still be here,' Mad Bill said. 'If you want to take your chances with the rats in that tunnel, you three go right ahead.'

'Rats?' Hendrik said. 'That's what you said about this place.'

'I just know deeper in there are rats. I told you the smell of the candles keep them away from this end of the tunnel. But you can bet your life, literally, they're waiting somewhere in the shadows to get their revenge.' He put on a Darth Vader voice. 'You killed my father.'

Hendrik thrust out his jaw. 'Well, I'm game.' He looked from Davy to Ralph.

Davy looked down at his bare feet. 'If I still had my boots, I might give it a shot.'

'What about you, Ralph? Wanna run the gauntlet in those running shoes?'

'Me? I have a pregnant wife and an unborn child I'd like to see one day. That won't happen if rats have chewed out both my eyeballs.'

'You're both wimps.' Hendrik threw up his hands.

He decided to go it alone but he didn't get far.

He had to shift some boxes that blocked his way, and when he saw what was inside, he realised he had a better plan.

He returned to the chamber carrying a heavy box full of old radio equipment, which he put in front of the candle so he could inspect what was there.

'I think I can make this work,' he said, after rummaging through the box. 'I think all the parts I need are here.'

Shortly after, Davy found the stockpile of food.

This came as another surprise to Mad Bill who had known where to find the ammo, the crates where the 80-year-old sherry was, and the pallets where the gold bars were. But he had never even opened the boxes over the back before. In those, Davy found tins that had long lost their labels.

'Where'd you find those, sonny?' Mad Bill gasped when Davy came out with a tin in either hand. He shook them in turn and it was obvious by the sound there was something inside both of them.

'There are dozens of them back there in boxes,' Davy said. 'Some of the boxes are full of old tins of paint, but these are different. What do you reckon they are?'

'Bring them over here, and I'll open them and see.'

Mad Bill removed one of the tools from the wall. It might have been the biggest can-opener Ralph had ever seen, but probably it was a garden tool from the 1940s or 1950s. In any case, it did the job.

The first tin yielded a glutinous brown liquid. Mad Bill dipped his finger in it and tasted it. 'Dripping. No good without a bit of toast to put it on.'

He hit the jackpot with the second tin.

Mad Bill looked like he was in seventh-heaven when he sampled it. 'Oh yes, that's nice. A memory from my childhood. Bully beef.'

Ralph had never heard of bully beef. But it beat the hell out of snake. They washed it down with 80-year-old sherry.

To cap off a night of discovery, Ralph scavenged around the left-hand tunnel and found boxes of blankets and bedrolls.

THIRTY-FIVE
SONS OF PEACHES

RALPH HAD no idea what time it was. Mid-morning perhaps? It was hard to tell in the dim-ness.

They were sitting on the stone floor, backs against the wall, legs out.

They had just opened another tin, which appeared to contain some kind of stewed fruit, and they were passing it down the line.

Hendrik said it tasted like pears. Mad Bill, who had put his false teeth back in, was convinced it was peaches. Ralph was just about to raise the spoon to his lips when the clunk of the door attracted their attention.

They all turned to see Darkey's head peering in.

Then it disappeared as an echo came from beyond. 'Come get a load of this?'

'No way,' came the reply. By the sound of it Whitey was still halfway up the stairwell. 'Just tell me. Are they dead? Have the rats eaten bits of them?'

'Come see for yourself. Ain't no rats I can see.'

'Are you sure?' Whitey said.

'Give me credit. I know what a rat looks like.'

The clip-clop noise told them Whitey was coming to the bottom. His face supplanted Darkey's at the door.

'Well, looky here.' Whitey blew air from his cheeks. 'They survived the night.'

He opened the door and entered, still holding the handgun. Following was Darkey, now armed with the old shotgun. Whether he had found ammo, who knew? The thing was when someone coined the phrase *tooled up*, they probably didn't have a giant spanner in their mind's eye. Now he looked like a proper crim.

By the time they stood over the captives, Ralph had passed the tin to Davy because he had suddenly lost his appetite. Whitey leant down and swiped it from his hands and the tin clattered as it bounced way across the stone floor, leaving a trail of pear/peach slurry behind it.

'It sure stinks in here as bad as it stinks upstairs.' He sniffed. Three times.

Then he walked over and kicked the can from where it had come to a standstill. 'But while we've been upstairs eating snake and fucking fruit loops and corn flakes, it looks to me these boys have had access to gourmet food down here.'

He looked Ralph in the eye and snarled: 'You told me there were rats down here, lots of rats.'

Ralph pointed to Mad Bill next to him. 'Well, that's what he told me.'

Mad Bill turned shrill. 'I tell everyone that in order to safeguard my stuff.' He pointed to one of the tunnels, which Ralph had been willing him not to point out, thinking it might just be their way out of here after all.

But then Ralph realised Whitey had no reason to even suspect it was a tunnel. He probably thought it was some kind of storeroom, because there were stacks of boxes in view. Same with the other tunnel.

'What kind of stuff do you feel the need to safeguard?'

'Do you have to wave that gun at me? You want the bullet to ricochet off the walls and kill you too?'

Whitey lowered the gun. 'OK, but I'm warning you.' He turned to Darkey, who still had the shotgun poised.

'He's no threat when he hasn't got ammo,' Mad Bill said.

'Willing to take that risk, are you? How do you know we didn't find some?'

'I know because I don't keep ammo upstairs.' He pointed to the darkened entrance again. 'I keep it all over there.'

All Ralph could think was: *Good one, Mad Bill, why don't you tell him about the gold?*

He must have read his mind, because the very next thing he said was: 'The ammo's in the boxes in front of the gold ingots.'

'Gold?' Whitey said. 'Why would there be gold?'

He looked sideways at Darkey. 'I thought you said you had already staked this place out? "Nothing here but a hermit with no phone?"'

'He was right about me having no phone,' Mad Bill said. He pointed to the radio dials and boxes with aerials Hendrik had spent the night assembling. 'I didn't know that lot was just sitting down here though. Hendrik is confident he can get it all going and ask someone to send help.'

Hendrik stared at the old man and gasped. 'Why'd you have to go and tell him that?'

'Well, it's plain for them to see. If you hadn't kept us awake half the night …'

Hendrik looked like he hurt more than when he had blood streaming down his head. 'You stupid old goat.'

Whitey sniffed and waved the gun at Hendrik. 'Do you want another taste of this?' He smiled. 'If anyone is going to call that old man stupid, it's me.'

Darkey started laying into the radio equipment with the butt of the shotgun. Whitey stood in front of Hendrik sniffing and grinning and daring him to just try him. If Mad Bill and Ralph hadn't been flanking him they wouldn't have been able to hold him back either — and it probably would have resulted in more gun butt blows raining down on his head.

'What do you think you are doing?' Hendrik said, as the metal began to crunch and the glass dials began to shatter. 'I nearly had that radio going. It was the ticket out of here — for all of us.'

Whitey just sniffed and smiled some more as he watched the angst in Hendrik's eyes and heard the noisy demolition job behind him. 'Oops. Didn't I tell you, Darkey, to be careful with that sensitive equipment?'

Hendrik looked like he was about to cry.

'You should have stuck to Plan A,' Mad Bill said. 'If you had escaped in the tunnel, you'd be near to the mainland by now.'

THIRTY-SIX
OUT WITH THE RATS AND SNAKES

MAD BILL and his big mouth! The tunnels might have become a real escape option had Whitey and Darkey locked them in that place for another night, having first removed all the food, the sherry, the gold, the bedding and even the foul-smelling candles.

But now they knew the tunnels might just go to the mainland, Plan A disappeared.

Darkey made certain of that sad fact after he went searching for the cache of ammo. He came out of the first tunnel looking like a cobweb-covered Rambo, with belts of cartridges draped over both shoulders.

'He's right, Whitey. It looks like it's a tunnel. It just seems to go on and on till you can't see where it goes no more.'

'Did you see the gold?'

'No, but it's dark, and there are all kinds of boxes back there.'

Whitey pointed the gun at Mad Bill again. 'You better not be lying to me, old man.'

'Didn't I tell you not to point that at me? You really have a death wish, don't you?'

'You got that right. You just don't know who's death I'm wishing for.' He waved the gun. 'Come on, get up. All of you. And don't try anything.'

With Rambo in tow, he ushered them at gunpoint out the door and up the stairs.

They all had to shield their eyes with their hands when they hit the daylight streaming through the window.

'What are we going to do with them now?' Darkey said.

'I reckon a night out in the open where we know there are *real* rats and *real* snakes might be the ticket,' Whitey said.

THIRTY-SEVEN
AND STAY OUT UNTIL YOU'RE DEAD

WHITEY AND DARKEY pushed their captives out the front door.

'And stay out until you're dead.' Whitey said.

Davy broke into a smile when the big metal door had slammed closed. 'They've let us go!'

'Go where exactly?' Hendrik said. 'We're stuck on an island, remember? Thanks to big mouth here ...' he put a hand on Mad Bill's head as they walked, '... we have no chance of radioing for help.'

Then his face brightened as something dawned on him. 'Unless ...?'

'Unless what?' Ralph said.

'I bet those clowns didn't know the life-raft they used has an EPIRB on board?'

'What's an EPIRB?'

'It stands for Emergency Position Indicating Radio Beacon. If we can find it and activate it, it'll transmit our position for 48 hours. The Australian Maritime Safety Authority will pick it up and send a helicopter to rescue us.'

Mad Bill frowned. 'But I don't want to be rescued. I just want everyone off my island, especially any black people.'

Ralph grabbed Davy's wrist and held his arm up. 'Does he look black to you?'

'It's hard to tell with all those tattoos,' the old man said.

'Blue is not the new black,' Ralph said. Then he lifted Hendrik's arm. 'Well, does *his* skin look dark?'

'If Michael Jackson could make himself white, anyone can change their skin colour.'

By this time, they had walked to the cemetery. Mad Bill and Ralph sat down on the bench, and Davy and Hendrik sat on the low wall on the other side of the gravestones.

Ralph squinted against the sun. 'How do you even know about Wacko Jacko anyway?'

'Darkey used to bring me magazines with the mail. My favourite was *Pig Shooting Monthly* but sometimes I had to settle for celebrity gossip mags.' Mad Bill looked sideways and frowned. 'Do you know who else is dead?'

Ralph scratched his head. 'Jimi Hendrix?'

'Again? I thought he had already died before I came out here.'

'I can't believe you told Darkey and Whitey about the gold?' Ralph said.

'No point trying to hide it from them. Scallywags like those fellas would have found out sooner or later. Shame I didn't win that seat in the Senate. I was going to lobby for the return of the electric chair.'

'You do know that Australian never actually had the electric chair.'

'You sure?'

'Even hanging was stopped in 1967.'

'Well, I was going to try to do a deal with the greenies. I'm sure they'd come at the idea of the electric chair if we could power it with renewable energy.'

Ralph raked his forehead with his fingers. 'How would you even know about solar power and wind power?'

'Why wouldn't I? You think all the articles in *Pig Shooting Monthly* are about pig shooting?'

Ralph rolled his eyes. 'If only someone knew we were here. If the police knew Whitey and Darkey were here they'd probably drop a SWOT team in to arrest them.'

Mad Bill put a finger to his lips. 'Keep your voice down, sonny. If that kind of word gets out, the real estate prices in this neighbourhood will plummet.'

'I thought you didn't want to sell?'

'It might force my hand. I came here to get away from people like that. The last thing I want to do is live in a high crime area.'

Ralph rose. 'Well, let's find this life-raft. Davy, if you and Hendrik go that way, Mad Bill and I will go round the island anti-clockwise. It shouldn't be too hard to find a big yellow raft.'

Wrong. They came back together 10 minutes later, all of them shaking our heads, and Davy and Hendrik complaining about getting prickles in their feet. Where the hell had Whitey and Darkey hidden the raft?

THIRTY-EIGHT
DEATH WATCH

RALPH SAT DOWN on the bench again and put his head in his hands. 'What are we going to do now?'

Mad Bill put a hand on his shoulder. 'I reckon we've landed on our feet.'

'How do you figure that?'

'Whitey and Darkey don't know we have an endless supply of food and water out here. We can get to the veggie garden and the well.' He pointed towards Davy. 'I bet that tattooed monkey can climb the trees and get us some coconuts.' He cackled. 'We even know where the big tree is; they don't.'

He stopped laughing when Ralph said they were probably using the old toilet in the pantry. He was obviously thinking of the detrimental effect it might have on further real estate evaluation.

Hendrik thumbed towards the house. 'I just bet they're using the life-raft in there as an air mattress.'

'What's this EPIRB thingy look like? Won't they twig?' Ralph said.

'Darkey might, I doubt Whitey will. They mightn't have even seen it. It was packed in a protective heat-sealed plastic bag. There was also food and water in that bag but the EPIRB was covered with packing foam.'

Ralph instinctively looked at his watch, but just reminded him he had taken his first swim at 3.52pm.

'Anyone have any idea of the time?' he asked.

Davy and Hendrik, who were sitting on the wall again, shook their heads. This was no surprise. Ralph knew their watches had seized up in the water too.

Mad Bill looked at his fob watch again. 'It's seventeen-and-a-half past noon.'

'You had that watch in your pocket all last night! You could have told us.'

'Nobody asked.'

Ralph rolled his eyes. 'I know you said our food, drink and toileting needs were sorted, but have you spared a thought about our sleeping arrangements?'

Mad Bill slapped the timber of the park-bench seat beside him. 'I often sleep right here when it gets too hot to sleep inside.'

Ralph screwed up his face. 'I can't sleep in a graveyard.'

'Why not? It's the living buggers you have to worry about. Would you prefer to take your chances with those scallywags in the house?'

'What about the rats and the snakes? Every time I'd close my eyes, I'd imagine their beady little eyes fixed on me.'

'You don't need to worry about that.' Mad Bill shrugged. 'Neither the rats nor the snakes ever come near this graveyard. Don't know what it is.' He pointed to the nearest headstone. 'Maybe they can smell the disease these people died from.'

THIRTY-NINE
THE GREAT UNWASHED

HENDRIK LIFTED HIS RIGHT ARM, and sniffed, and then did the same with his left. 'What's the best way for a bloke to bathe around here?'

Three sets of eyes locked on to Mad Bill.

He shrugged. 'I normally wait until the sea temperature is warmer. Can't you wait another month or two?'

Hendrik looked like that painting of The Scream. 'No, I can't wait. And it's not just me. We're all starting to pong.' He glared at Mad Bill. 'You especially.'

Mad Bill looked affronted. 'I've never had any complaints before.'

Hendrik rolled his eyes. 'Are you trying to tell me you only wash once a year?'

'Course not. Sometimes we have four or five really hot days in a row.'

'When was the last really hot day?'

Mad Bill fixed his sight on a nearby coconut tree. 'Hmm, late February.'

'And you haven't bathed since?'

'Why would I? I told you: no-one has complained.'

Hendrik used his fingers to count the months the old man hadn't washed. 'Jesus!'

This is how they came to all go down to the little beach on the north side of the island.

Mad Bill finally agreed to remove his shirt and rolled up his pants so he could wade out a bit. He stooped down and splashed some water over his scrawny arms and torso that clearly showed all his ribs.

Hendrik, Davy and Ralph went in fully clothed.

The water was warm and it felt good to feel clean again.

They dined on raw carrots after their swim/bath. Davy jokingly said the carrots would at least enhance their eyesight at night should Mad Bill's theory be wrong that the rats and the snakes would leave them alone.

After eating, they checked the undergrowth around the fringe of the island but after drawing another blank concluded the life-raft, and the EPIRB with it, had probably been taken inside.

Hendrik tried to look at the bright side. 'Maybe Whitey will roll on it during the night and set it off.'

As the sun sunk into the ocean, they sat around the gravestones talking and fielding possible escape plans.

'Perhaps we could *build* a raft,' Davy said.

'We've got no idea how long that voyage might take,' Hendrik said. 'What would we do for food?'

'You can take some of my carrots with you,' Mad Bill said.

'Good idea. That would keep us from getting scurvy,' Davy said.

'I don't know about you?' Hendrik glared at him. 'But when they find me dead on a raft floating aimlessly, I don't want them to find at the post-mortem the last thing I ate in this life was a carrot!'

Ralph glanced at Mad Bill, who was reclining on the bench. 'You wouldn't come on the raft with us?'

'Are you crazy? I told you. The current would just take you past Tasmania and down to the Antarctic. Too cold for me. Besides, I want to see Whitey's and Darkey's faces when they realise you three have escaped.'

'Wouldn't you be scared?' Ralph said. 'Whitey is a psychopath and he seems to have Darkey wrapped around his trigger finger.'

'No, I've said it before. I'm just about ready to check out anyway. I'd just change my will. I'd make *them* bury me. They'd be breaking the law of this island if they didn't honour my wishes.'

Mad Bill got up and went to one of the headstones, wriggling free its plaque. Inside was a cavity, from which he pulled a bunch of candles and a box of matches.

Hendrik was beside himself.

'We have the moon and the stars to give us light. Why do we need those foul-smelling things again? Out here in the fresh air?'

Mad Bill shrugged. 'Please yourself, but don't blame me if a rat nibbles on your feet in the night.'

'I thought you said the rats and the snakes won't come near this place. That they can still detect the smell of the people buried here?'

'That's right. But my other theory is they just don't like the smell of the candles.' He pursed his lips to say something else but the other three said it for him in three-part Darth Vader harmony: 'You killed my father.'

Mad Bill didn't seem to appreciate them stealing his limelight. 'Call that singing?' He waggled an outstretched index finger. 'I just hope Whitey and Darkey can harmonise better when they have to sing *Hallelujah* at my funeral.'

He took a candle over to the ledge and lit it.

'Time for some shut-eye,' Mad Bill said.

That was easy for him to say. Ralph couldn't speak for Hendrik and Davy, but he had trouble getting to sleep with the rats hissing and fighting out there in the dark. He couldn't actually hear the snakes but he knew they were out there too.

FORTY
SO YOU'RE NOT DEAD!

RALPH WOKE with the heat of the early morning sun beating down on his face, and opened his eyes to see the barrel of a gun pointing at his face.

'So you're not dead?' Whitey sniffed, and adjusted his grip on the yellow rubber duck in his left hand. 'That's a stroke of luck, as it happens.'

From his position on the ground, Ralph could see Darkey had the shotgun trained on Hendrik and Davy, who were now sitting up. How Mad Bill kept snoring away on the bench, heaven knows? You'd think a hermit would be sensitive to the slightest noise, but perhaps it worked the other way around. His false teeth were beside him on the ground.

'We thought the rats and the snakes would have made a meal of you boys overnight,' Whitey said. 'What's your secret? The old man's snoring scared them away?'

Whitey started laughing like a percolator nearing the boil, then Darkey joined him. I could see now Darkey had the other rubber duck at his feet.

Their combined noise was enough to awaken Mad Bill, who gurgled and snorted himself awake.

Whitey stopped laughing. 'So nice of you to join us, old man. I was just saying how you fellows led a charmed life. I would have bet all my gold you'd all have some decent-sized chunks bitten out of you last night.'

'My gold, you mean?'

'Your gold? I don't think so! Tell you what? I'll let you say goodbye to it after you help load it.'

'Load it? Load it on what?'

'The trolley you boys are going to build today. I thought we were going to have to build it ourselves so imagine how pleasantly surprised we were to find you all still in one piece. We only came out to do a bit of target practice with the ducks.'

'They're my ducks!' cried Davy.

'Bullshit,' Whitey said. 'You didn't have any ducks when you left the boat.'

'I found them at sea. They saved my life, so they have great sentimental value. Please don't hurt them.'

Whitey mimicked him in a child's voice. '*Please don't hurt my duckies. They have great sentimental value.*'

He looked over to Darkey. 'Wouldn't want to separate a man from his fucking ducks, would we?'

He looked back to the deckhand. 'Tell you what, Davy boy …' He threw his duck at him and motioned for him to fetch the other one. '… You can help us with target practice.'

He pointed to the big tree. 'You just go stand over there, a duck in either hand stretched out as far as you can. If the sights on this gun are accurate, I should be able to hit both ducks from this distance. If I miss and kill you instead, oops, sorry.'

FORTY-ONE
DEAD DUCKS

THEY CLOSED their eyes when Whitey took aim.

They only opened them after they heard screams after two rapid shots.

The good news was that Whitey had hit his targets and Davy was still upright.

But he was rocking back and forwards with both hands tucked in their opposite armpits, the disfigured yellow blobs either side of him on the ground.

Whitey bent over with laughter, gasping something about shitting ducks. Then he rose to his full height and his smile transformed to a smirk. 'Playtime is over, boys. It's time for you lot to go to work.'

Davy was unable to even raise his burned hands as they were marched back towards the house. Goodness knows how he managed to get down the narrow stairs without grabbing the side wall for balance?

Ralph really hadn't expected to be back in this cellar.

'We're not greedy,' Whitey said when they had lined up against the wall again. 'But we're going to have to take the gold with us.'

'If you think I'm going to help you get away with my own gold...?'

Whitey pointed the gun at Mad Bill. 'You'll do what exactly?'

'I told you. Don't go firing that thing in here, sonny. No telling whose head might get the ricochet bullet. Yours hopefully! Anyway, the only thing I'm good at making is snake pie.'

Whitey turned his gaze on to Hendrik.

'Don't look at me,' the skipper said. 'Davy is the one who's good with his hands, or he was until you used them for target practice. I'm pretty good at navigating and finding fish and tinkering with radio equipment, but don't go expecting me to put things together in an orderly fashion. My mind just doesn't work that way.'

Whitey turned to Ralph. 'Looks like it's up to you, reporter boy? And if you know what's good for you, don't start telling me you're no good at handyman things too.'

This is why Ralph didn't.

He didn't tell him about the school football trophy he accidentally welded to a bench in metalwork. He expected the school was still trying to work that one out. You're not supposed to be able to weld wooden bases.

Ralph looked at the pram again and an incredible sadness came over him. He and Maria hadn't got around to buying a pram for the baby yet, and here was he about to cannibalise a Mary Poppins pram. It just didn't seem right.

FORTY-TWO
LOVE ME KNOT

RALPH COULD SEE Davy's red, swollen hands weren't going to be any help.

But Hendrik surely could lend a hand.

'I'm sorry, I doubt I can be any use to you.' Hendrik said. 'I was born without the handyman gene. My skill has always been to surround myself with practical people.' He shrugged. 'I can tie knots. Will that be any assistance?'

It turned out it was.

Ralph found enough timber in the tunnels to make a platform, which he nailed it all together using nails he extracted from scattered crates. But the only way he could think of securing the wheels to the axles was with some rope he found hanging on the wall in one of the tunnels.

'Are you sure this will hold?' Hendrik tied it all down with a reef knot.

'Can't see why not?' Ralph was so proud of himself for his ingenuity he did a little happy dance while singing a cheerful ditty he also made up.

Darkey stood up and pointed the shotgun at Ralph. 'Will you shut the fuck up!' He fixed his gaze on the trolley. 'That doesn't look very secure to me.'

Darkey had been left to watch over them. The hoods had relocated a card table and two chairs from upstairs. Whitey had taken Mad Bill upstairs to supervise him while he was making lunch.

Ralph realised while he was rummaging around in one of the tunnels looking for spare parts that all the sherry was gone.

Hopefully, it wouldn't be too hard to find the stash after the hoods had made their escape through the tunnel.

Ralph, Hendrik and Mad Bill would need some liquid refreshment after they had loaded all that gold on the trolley.

After quenching their thirst all they would have to do was find the life-raft, which had to be in the house somewhere, set off the rescue beacon and wait for help to arrive.

Ralph didn't predict what Darkey would say next though.

'Seeing as you're so clever, da Vinci, is there any way to incorporate a life-raft in your design?'

'Which life-raft?'

'Which one do you think? We'll need the yellow life-raft to sleep in if it turns out to be a long tunnel.'

Ralph scratched his head. 'Do you think the tunnel will be wide enough? That raft is pretty big.'

Darkey examined the entrance to the tunnel. 'It looks wide enough to me.'

'It might narrow.'

'We'll take that chance. I'm more worried how long it is. It took us 24 hours or so to get here, and that was in a boat that goes a lot faster than a trolley full of gold and a life-raft we will have to pull.'

'We're actually a lot closer to land than you think,' Hendrik said quickly.' It only seems we're a long way from it because we tracked up the coast so far. So why carry the extra burden of the life-raft?'

'You don't get it, do you? If we leave it here, you know Whitey's going to want to kill you all. He won't want you using it to escape this island. You boys should be thanking me. I persuaded Whitey to take the raft with us and let you all live.'

Ralph and Hendrik looked at each other.

'There's a trade-off though.' Darkey said. 'Whitey knows if we take the life-raft, there'll be no room for all that sherry. But you know what he's like? If he can't have it, there's no way he's going to let you have it.'

'What do you mean?' Ralph asked.

Darkey shook his head. 'It took us hours to take it all upstairs last night but that was before we decided to had to get out of here. The plan had been to drink them one by one and use the empty bottles for target practice. Now they're going to have to be full when I rake them with a few shotgun blasts.'

Ralph and Hendrik looked at each other again.

Hendrik said: 'What's to stop us just following you to freedom in the tunnel?'

'Whitey has already thought of that. He's going to wait at the other end with his gun.'

'For how long?'

Darkey shrugged. 'I guess that's for you to find out.'

FORTY-THREE
REPTILE STEW

MAD BILL APPEARED CARRYING a big bowl of steaming snake stew.

Behind him was Whitey, who carried a tray with a bunch of spoons, empty bowls, a carton of long-life milk and a Variety Breakfast Cereal Pack. It didn't take much guessing the Rice Bubbles were for them and the reptile stew was for the captives.

Since Davy still couldn't hold a spoon, Mad Bill took it upon himself to spoon-feed him. As if Ralph needed another reminder of what he soon might be missing with a baby in the house! 'Now close your eyes and open your mouth,' the old man said.

When Mad Bill had given Davy his fill (careful to scrape every recalcitrant drop of white sauce from his lips and into his mouth while simultaneously making brom-brom noises), he turned his attention to his own bowl. Ralph had rarely seen such hungry eating.

'What?' he said, when he saw everyone looking. 'I have to make the most of it because at my age you never know when your last meal will be!'

Whitey's angry voice rose above them. 'If you don't shut up, old man, that *will* be your last meal.'

Both he and Darkey were sitting at the card table, and were both bent over their bowls.

'I can't hear the snap, crackle and pop over that noise,' Whitey said.

'That'll be the least of your worries if you steal my gold.'

Whitey sat up straight and pointed his spoon, as if he thought he was still holding his gun. 'It ain't your gold though, is it, old man? You found it here after you arrived on this island?'

'Possession is nine-tenths of the law.'

Whitey looked at Darkey and smiled. 'That's the same principle *we* use.'

'So you're prepared to run the gauntlet of rats in that tunnel?' Mad Bill said.

'Do you really think we're stupid, old man?' Whitey said. 'You said there were rats down here. Why? I'll tell you why. You thought that story would keep your gold and sherry safe? Well, it didn't work. And that whopper of a lie might just get you dead.'

'You think that worries me? If I die tomorrow I'm still 60-odd years up on you. But if rats kill you in that tunnel …'

'Oh, I look *real* scared.'

'You should be. Why do you think I've been on this island so long? No way would I risk my life trying to get through that tunnel.'

Whitey sniffed his brains back in once more.

He laughed at his little witticism to come. 'I reckon the reason you speak with forked tongue is you've eaten too many snakes.'

His smile turned into a scowl. 'Now be a good old man and go open one of those cans. Let's see how good you are finding the apricots.'

Turns out he was no good at it at all. When Mad Bill opened the can, he was faced with the dark glutinous liquid. More dripping!

FORTY-FOUR
CHITTY CHITTY BOONG BOONG

MAD BILL TOLD Whitey he was welcome to pick some food from the veggie patch for the trip.

'Do I look like a fucking rabbit?'

'As a matter of fact …' Mad Bill cleared his throat to give him time to think what he was going to say instead of what he seemed to be thinking,'… vegetables are a good source of vitamins and minerals.'

Whitey pointed to the boxes of gold bars in the tunnel entrance. 'I reckon I have all the minerals I'll ever need right in there.' He showed his yellow teeth again. 'Gold is a mineral, right?'

He scooped up another spoonful of rich bubbles.

'Sorry about the missing toys, sonny,' Mad Bill said.

Whitey hadn't quite raised the spoon to his mouth. 'Sorry about the what?'

'They used to put toys in boxes of breakfast cereal. Little brightly colour plastic critters'

Whitey looked at him blankly. 'When?'

'Years ago. This batch hasn't got them though. They stopped doing it because they came to realise the toys were a potential choking hazard. Pity.'

Whitey squinted. It was a mean squint. 'Are you trying to be smart with me?' He waved his spoon again and this time the cereal went snap, crackle, plop as soggy Rice Bubbles scattered across the concrete floor. 'The only thing keeping you alive, old man, is I need you to load the gold now that Davy has hurt his little girly hands.'

For those of you who have never had to lift a gold ingot (which was Ralph's own precise experience before this day) they are heavy. Ralph wondered how on earth Mad Bill had managed to haul them upstairs one by one to pay various door-to-door salesmen. The way the old man huffed and puffed every time he tried to lift a gold bar on to the trolley just deepened the mystery.

It was a testament Ralph's wobbly handyman skills the trolley held up well until the seventh gold ingot made the structure begin to sag. By the time they loaded the twelfth gold bar he knew they were in trouble.

It was the sixteenth gold bar that did it in. One minute the trolley was holding together well despite the strain, the next the pram wheels flopped almost horizontally to the stone floor like the fold-down wheels on Chitty Chitty Bang Bang, another happy childhood memory Ralph would probably never be able to pass on to his new daughter.

Whitey leapt to his feet. 'I thought you said you were a decent handyman.'

'I never said that,' Ralph said. 'Davy is the only proper handyman among us. But look at him …' They had found some bandages for his hands in Mad Bill's first-aid kit and he was sitting in the corner feeling sorry for himself. 'If you hadn't injured him!'

Whitey pointed his gun. 'Are you trying to make me angry!'

'It's not my fault.' Ralph looked at the flattened trolley. 'I guess we can fix it but you're going to have to do two trips. And forget about us putting the life-raft on top. That thing will just be too heavy.'

'Journalist boy, you don't seem to comprendo,' Whitey snarled. 'No way are we making two trips. You have to remake that thing to take *all* the gold and when we bring the raft down in the morning it has to take the weight of that too.'

'But what if we can't get it to work?'

'I guess if that pans out like that I'm gonna have to kill you.' He sniffed like he meant it.

Hendrik and Ralph got back to work. This time the skipper tied a double reef knot. 'Let's see that one come untied.'

FORTY-FIVE
QUIET AS A GRAVEYARD

'OUT WITH THE rats for the night.' With a wave of his shotgun, Darkey herded them outside and slammed the door behind them.

'We're free again.' Davy sounded a lot more cheerful.

'You still don't get it, do you?' Hendrik pointed to the ground as they walked towards the graveyard. 'The only way off this island is through the tunnels now we can't get our hands on the EPIRB.'

'Maybe they'll simply have to leave it here because it's too heavy?' Ralph said.

'It hardly matters,' Hendrik said. 'Even if the trolley holds the extra weight, my guess is we're surplus to Whitey's requirements.' He raised a hand and pointed to his head. 'Bang, bang.'

A look of alarm came over Davy. 'But Darkey said—'

'I don't give a rat's arse what Darkey said,' Hendrik said. 'Whitey clearly calls the shots. Literally!'

Whoever coined the expression *quiet as a graveyard* might want to redefine it. Ralph was sure they took silence down to new levels as they sat down around the headstones, contemplated the end of their lives and summoned up cherished memories.

Davy, Hendrik and Ralph sat on the wall, leaving the bench to Mad Bill, who was lying on his back looking up to the sky.

Ralph didn't have time to guess what the other blokes were thinking. He was too busy summoning up images of Maria's smiling face and her swollen belly.

Davy was the first to speak. Judging by the way he waved his hands, the circulation had returned. 'We've got to do something? We just can't let them shoot us dead. Surely we can hide?'

'Where are we going to hide on this tiny island?' Hendrik said.

'We could hide in the veggie patch.' Ralph tried to lighten the mood. 'Whitey would never think to look there.'

'I think he'd see through the fact we're not really carrots.' Hendrik looked over to Mad Bill. 'You're quiet?'

'I have a lot more memories than you youngsters to flash before my eyes!' The old man exhaled wheezily and turned on to his side to face the others. 'But it's a relief in a way. I've spent my life wondering how it's going to end. Now I know.'

Davy spat on the ground next to him. 'Well, I don't intend to take this lying down. Anyone got a better idea than hiding?'

Mad Bill said: 'All the best hiding spots are inside the house.'

Hendrik looked the old man in the eyes. 'Played a lot of hide-and-seek, have you?'

'You can laugh, but there are places to hide in that house you'd never think of looking in.'

'Really?' This gave Ralph an idea.

As the sun went down, and Mad Bill lit those foul-smelling candles again, he told them what he had come up with.

They talked it through and developed it into an actual plan.

They would rise at the crack of dawn, hide on the other side of the house and when the hoods came out to force them inside, they would sneak through the door and hide. Mad Bill prepped them well. They divvied up all the best hiding spots he told them about. If the plan worked, Whitey and Darkey would eventually give up looking for them and just leave, taking the 24 bars of gold, which was already loaded on the trolley, with them into the tunnel and leaving behind the all-important emergency beacon so they could summon rescuers.

Mad Bill started cackling. 'I half hope they find my hiding place though. I'd sure hate to lose all that gold.'

'You really can't take it with you, you silly old goat!' Hendrik said.

'Why not? I might need it where I'm going.' He cackled again. 'Just before Whitey shoots me, I'm going to hand him an envelope containing my last will and testament. My only regret is that I won't be around to see his face when he rips it open and realises he's compelled to bury all the gold with me.'

FORTY-SIX
FIGURED IT OUT, HAVE YOU?

RALPH WOKE when a flashlight was shone in his face. 'There's been a change of plans, boys.' Darkey's voice came beating down with a spray of spittle.

Ralph raised himself from the ground and rubbed his eyes. 'What time is it?'

He could still hear Mad Bill snoring. Did he always sleep like the dead, or just in this place?

'What's it matter to you what time it is? Whitey and I haven't even been to bed yet.'

Ralph shaded his eyes with a hand. 'Where'd you get that flashlight from?'

Darkey stepped into the flickering candlelight. He had the flashlight in one hand and held the shotgun limply with the other. 'This?' He held it up. 'It was one of the things we found in the survival bag on the raft. Food too! We ate better at sea than we have done since we've been on this fucking island.'

'You can say that again,' came Whitey's voice from the shadows.

Hendrik sighed. If he had been playing chess, Ralph reckoned he was about ready to knock his king over in resignation. 'So you must have found the EPIRB too?'

Darkey turned to the darkness where no doubt Whitey was standing pointing his gun at one of them.

Ralph could see by Darkey's body language that he was feeling embarrassed. 'I should have twigged earlier what that yellow thing was.' He turned back to Hendrik. 'When I found it on the life-raft I assumed it was one of those first-generation mobile phones — the size of a brick and typical of a cheapskate like you, skipper. I knew we were never going to get reception out in the middle of the ocean.'

Hendrik was on his feet now. 'Christ, you've been working on boats for years. You must have known it was an emergency beacon!'

'But this was my first time on a life-raft. You never had survival drills, you penny-pinching bastard!' He put the little flashlight in his top pocket and pointed to Davy. 'That's how come you never even knew he couldn't swim.'

'Who grows up on the coast and doesn't learn to swim?'

Davy was up and dusting himself off now. 'Darkey's right, skipper. You could have got me killed.'

'What's it matter?' The force of Hendrik's voice dropped. 'We're all going to die now anyway.'

Laughter came from the shadows. 'Figured it out, have you?' There was a sniffing noise, then a spitting noise, then the sound of phlegm hitting the ground.

Darkey turned to the shadows again. 'You said we'd spare them!'

'You think I like it? Sometimes murder just becomes an occupational hazard you can't avoid. You're talking like I have some kind of choice. Go on, tell these boys why they have to die a day earlier than I had planned.'

Darkey drew a deep breath and exhaled. Who knew they put garlic in sherry and breakfast cereal?

Darkey addressed Hendrik as if he were asking a teacher something he knew he really should know. 'What would you have to do to activate this emergency beacon of yours?'

'Two ways! You can set it going by flicking a switch. Or it activates automatically if it comes in contact with water.'

Darkey hung his head. 'Shit! That would account for it flashing.'

There was stunned silence. Even the snoring stopped. All Ralph could hear was the gentle crashing of the waves on the shore and the crackle of the burning candles.

That just didn't make sense.

Why would Darkey manually set the EPIRB off?

'Tell them, Darkey!' Whitey said.

'It wasn't my fault.' Darkey turned to the shadows. 'You were the one who said it was OK to use that toilet in the pantry.'

'I'm not a plumber.'

'Well, it wasn't hard to see something was wrong with it. If you had listened to me, we would never have started getting rats in the house.'

'You let rats into my house?' This is when they knew Mad Bill was actually awake. 'Do you know how long it took me to get those rats back outside.'

Another sniff. Another spit. 'Won't matter to you soon, old man.'

Mad Bill shrieked: 'What's he talking about?'

'When we started seeing the rats, numb-nuts here came up with the plan to store all the 80-year-old sherry in the life-raft and zip it up to keep the bottles safe,' Whitey said. 'I asked him: what are you doing that for? I'd never even heard of rats opening bottles. But no. He didn't listen to me. Worse, he broke one of the bottles.'

Darkey stamped his foot. 'It's not like I did it deliberately. If I had known about this emergency beacon, I wouldn't have stacked the bottles anywhere near it.'

Whitey stepped into the light. 'Fuck knows how long that thing has been going off? If we had done more drinking and less chin-wagging I would have found it sooner. But when I unzipped the raft to get another bottle, the thing was just blinking at me. Shit!'

Hendrik started laughing.

Whitey pointed the gun at him. 'Go ahead and laugh. You don't know what pleasure I'll have wiping the smile off your ugly, fat face.'

'You have to admit, that's one hell of a marketing hook.' Hendrik slapped his knee. 'Not only does this EPIRB activate when it comes into contact with sea water, 80-year-old sherry will also work.'

FORTY-SEVEN
MARIA WILL NEVER KNOW

THEY WERE MARCHED at gunpoint down into the foul-smelling basement.

Ralph couldn't stop thinking this is how Tsar Nicholas Romanov and his family had died in 1918 — exterminated by a hail of bullets in a basement. At least, their bodies were taken away and burnt in a forest. Ralph wouldn't even have that farewell trip. He looked around at his tomb. Most likely he'd rot away in this basement, and Maria and their child would never know his final resting place, never have a proper place to bring flowers to.

Why hadn't they hidden last night? Would staying awake have killed them? But it seemed like not staying awake was going to.

Ralph thought about crash-tackling Whitey. Four against two, right? They couldn't kill them all! But he realised the first crash-tackler would run into deadly lead. Maybe the second wave had a chance? But that would be no consolation to him if he were already dead. Ralph held his breath and waited for someone else to sacrifice themselves. He picked Davy as the one most likely to get the appropriate rush of blood to the head.

He was wrong though. Perhaps Davy wasn't as stupid as he

seemed to be. Next thing Ralph knew Whitey was ordering them to line up against the wall.

Ralph could hear his own heart pounding and blood swishing around his head.

Whitey and Darkey raised their guns.

'It's been nice knowing you boys,' Whitey said.

Mad Bill cried: 'Wait!'

Whitey and Darkey lowered their guns. 'What is it, old man?' Darkey said.

'I just wanted to be sure you take a couple of candles with you.'

Darkey looked annoyed. 'We don't need candles, we've got the flashlight.'

Mad Bill said. 'A flashlight will be no protection against rats.'

Whitey looked even more annoyed. 'We've had this conversation before. If there were rats in that tunnel, we would have heard them. Hell, they would have come right out and eaten you all — and saved Darkey and me a job.'

'The only reason they don't come out is because of the candles.'

Whitey and Darkey raised their guns again.

'Wait!'

This time it was Hendrik. 'Is that a helicopter I hear?'

Ralph could hear the aircraft, too, but it didn't sound like a rotor to him. It sounded more like a fixed-wing aircraft

Hendrik looked over at him and winked in a way so Whitey and Darkey couldn't see. 'How long have they been using Blackhawks to do search and rescues? Probably full of sharp-shooters!'

Darkey and Whitey looked at each other. The blood drained from their faces.

'This must be your lucky day,' Whitey said.

They felt the best way to make a quick getaway was for all four of the captives to get behind the gold-laden trolley and give it an almighty push down the tunnel. They planned to ride it as far as it went, then pull it along with the ropes Hendrik had attached to the front.

Ralph half-expected them to fire some parting shots back down the tunnel, but they didn't. He figured they didn't want to trigger a cave-in.

'Good riddance to them,' Mad Bill said as they disappeared into the gloom. 'Only three to go. I can't wait for that helicopter to arrive.'

Hendrik looked him in the eye.

'You didn't really believe that story about me hearing the chopper?'

'You made that up?'

'Not exactly. But it sounded to me like a plane flying low over the island — most likely looking for us.' He started laughing. 'I can't wait to tell the blokes at the marina about the broken bottle of sherry that saved our lives.'

FORTY-EIGHT

THEY CAN'T MAKE ME GO, CAN THEY?

THEY LEFT the basement as soon as they were convinced Whitey and Darkey weren't coming back. Mad Bill stopped at the door and looked around.

'What are you doing?' Hendrik asked.

'I'm trying to work out where they put the key,' Mad Bill said.

'Don't worry about that. We haven't got time. We need to get outside so the search plane will see us when it does another swoop.'

Mad Bill scratched his head. 'If those scallywags return, I don't want to make it easy for them to come back on to the island.'

'Relax,' Hendrik said. 'They're not coming back when they think a SWOT team will be here waiting for them. Just leave it.'

Hendrik started bounding up the stairs, two at a time. Davy was right behind him.

Mad Bill was next, shaking his head, and Ralph brought up the rear.

'Silliest thing I've heard in years,' echoed Mad Bill as he started his slow ascent on the stone stairs. 'You can't land a plane on this island. It's too small.'

'No, but when they see this is where we are, they'd send a boat to pick us up,' Hendrik shouted back.

By the time Mad Bill and Ralph reached the lounge-room, Hendrik and Davy were gone. Outside, he presumed.

Mad Bill took in the surroundings. 'Never thought I'd see this room again.' He paused for a moment and scratched his beard. 'They can't make me go, can they?'

'I wouldn't think so,' Ralph said. 'But why would you want to stay here now with these bad memories?'

'Yeah, losing all those gold bars makes me sick. I just hope those two ratbags get their comeuppance. But I have to look on the good side. I still have my life, and I've still got my sherry. I really do want to see out my days on this island.'

Ralph shrugged. 'Your choice, I guess.'

'You'd better join your friends outside. I'll go upstairs to look for my sherry.'

FORTY-NINE

A ROCK SHOW

WHEN RALPH GOT OUTSIDE, he saw Hendrik and Davy were busy collecting big rocks.

'What are you doing?' he said when Davy came towards him carrying a boulder he had got from the shore. The rush of adrenalin hands had restored his hands.

'We're making a sign they'll see from the air.' Davy dropped the rock and it landed with a dull thud. 'Skipper wants it to say S.A.S.'

Ralph frowned. 'Don't you mean S.O.S.?'

Davy tugged his beard, which Ralph suspected looked a lot better than his itchy growth. 'You might be right. Beats me. All I know is if I was playing Scrabble, I wouldn't want to waste my S's like that.'

Hendrik's voice came from behind them. 'Since when did you play Scrabble, Dumbo?'

They turned to see he had arrived with another big rock. He was puffing. 'Where's the old man?'

'He went upstairs to find the sherry,' Ralph said.

'He'd better not touch the EPIRB.' Hendrik had panic in his voice. He dropped his rock and started running towards the house.

FIFTY
PUT. ME. DOWN.

DAVY AND RALPH followed with less speed. They didn't know what the hurry was all about. What on earth would divert Hendrik from his urgent quest to make a sign that could be seen from the air?

When they found Hendrik and Mad Bill next to the life-raft in an upstairs bedroom, it became obvious.

Hendrik was standing behind Mad Bill, but held him in the air by his suspenders. The old man was trying to throw backward punches and connecting only with air.

'Put. Me. Down,' he squealed. 'I haven't seen your beacon, sonny.'

'Why would they take it with them?' Hendrik shouted back.

'Why would I pinch it?'

'You said it yourself. You want people here to bury you. You don't want us to be rescued.'

'That's where you're wrong. I wouldn't let you bury me if you were the last person alive on this island. And I won't warn you again. Put. Me. Down.'

Ralph tried to intervene. 'What are you doing, Hendrik?'

The skipper plonked the old man down and put his hands on his hips. 'He's only gone and hidden the EPIRB. Probably turned it off too.'

'Why would I do that?' Mad Bill said in an even more tremulous voice than he normally had. 'Sooner you foreigners leave me alone, the happier I'll be.'

'Foreigners?' Hendrik's voice rose again. 'I'm a second-generation Australian.'

'I was born and bred here too,' Davy said. 'I can trace my ancestry back to the First Fleet. My great, great, great, great grandfather was from County Cork in Ireland.'

'I knew it,' Mad Bill said. 'I knew there was something about you. You're descended from convicts. That explains why your eyes are too close together.'

'Now hang on,' Ralph said, coming to Davy's defence. His eyes *were* a little close-set but that was beside the point.

'I wouldn't be too quick to talk if I were you,' Mad Bill said. 'Where did you say your wife was from? Poland? Puerto Rico? Pakistan?'

'Portugal.'

'Same difference. I know your kind. You want to populate the world with half-caste children.'

'I came up here to help you not to be insulted by you.'

'It wouldn't surprise me if you're working in cahoots with the other two scallywags. First, they take my gold, and next you'll take my sherry. An elderly citizen is not safe on his own island any more.'

'Do you really want another wedgie, you mad old man?' Hendrik growled. 'None of us is remotely interested in your sherry, we just want the EPIRB back. Where have you hidden it?'

'It wasn't here for me to steal.'

Before he could explain further, all our heads turned to the door.

Darkey staggered into the room, clutching his chest. He fell forwards to the floor and we could see there was a blood trail behind him.

FIFTY-ONE
WHITEY'S DEAD

IT WAS BAD. Real bad. Darkey had a bullet hole that gushed blood every time his heart beat.

They couldn't lift him on to the bed because Mad Bill's bed had been removed from the room, presumably to make room for the life-raft and all the sherry.

They eased Darkey on to his back on the floor and someone fetched a pillow. They tried to stem the bleeding with strips of sheet Mad Bill tore up, but the blood just kept coming.

'Whitey's dead,' Darkey gasped. 'We got attacked by rats as soon as we went around the first bend and the trolley collapsed.' Then he said. 'I'm so cold. So thirsty.'

Mad Bill reached into the raft and grabbed a bottle of sherry he handed down to Ralph, who was kneeling near Darkey's head. Ralph wasn't sure he was doing the right thing giving a dying man sherry, but he uncorked the bottle and lifted it to Darkey's lips.

He let him take a glug, then removed it.

'Whitey shot me but it wasn't his fault. It was dark where the rats attacked. So much hissing and biting, it seemed like there were hundreds of them.' He moved his head from side to side.

Suddenly blood came through his mouth, too, and oozed down his chin. 'When I managed to switch on my flashlight, I could see the rats had bitten off one of Whitey's ears.'

He reached for the sherry bottle.

Ralph helped it to his lips.

'I'm so cold,' he said.

Ralph turned to Mad Bill. 'Are there any blankets?'

The old man scurried to another room and Darkey continued to ramble.

'I think he was just trying to get those vicious little bastards off him. It wasn't his fault he shot me. A lesser man wouldn't even have been able to take aim because by this point the rats had chewed out his eyes. His last words to me were: "Run, run, get away." You believe that? He tried to save me.'

'Just try to relax,' Ralph said. 'Mad Bill's fetching you a blanket.'

'I'm cold,' Darkey said.

'I know.' Ralph looked around anxiously. 'Where is he?'

'I'm so thirsty.'

Ralph lifted the bottle back to his lips. He managed more of a sip than a glug this time.

'Whitey died a hero. You believe that? Do you think God will take that into account, give him some kind of good behaviour bond?'

'Perhaps,' Ralph said, but he didn't really believe it.

'I'm hoping God goes easy on me, too, on account of my own good deed.' The power in his voice was decreasing now and Ralph had to lean closer over to hear.

'What good deed was that, Darkey?'

He coughed up some more blood. 'I set that beacon off deliberately so Whitey would want to get out of here quickly. How was I to know he'd still want to kill you all?'

He turned his head from side to side. 'I made a mistake, didn't I?'

Mad Bill ran into the room. 'Here is the blanket. Buggers had moved them.'

Darkey lifted his head. 'Whitey didn't have nothing to do with moving the blankets. That was all down to me. That cupboard seemed like a good place to hide the EPIRB.'

'You!' Hendrik said. 'You hid it? Why? You had already turned it on. What did it matter where it was?'

'I turned it back off before I hid it,' Darkey whispered. 'I had to ensure we had enough time to escape. It would do us no good if you were rescued too soon.'

'And Whitey didn't know any of this?' Hendrik growled.

'Shit, no,' Darkey said. 'If Whitey had known I could actually turn the beacon off, he would have taken his time making you do a good job on the trolley, maybe even given Davy time to recover. Journalist boy here is obviously hopeless, Mad Bill is way past it and you've got to be the most inept tow-truck driver I've ever seen.'

Hendrik balled up his fists. Ralph stretched out his arms to shroud Darkey in some sort of protection.

'I ought to …'

'Ought to what? Kill me? Aren't you a bit late for that?'

'You're right,' Hendrik said.' All's well that ends well. At least we know where to find the beacon now?'

Darkey coughed up some more blood. 'Maybe, maybe not. I relocated it to another very good hiding spot.'

Hendrik grabbed the front of Darkey's collar and shook him. 'Where is it now, God damn it?'

The bald man stared into space.

It took them a minute or two to realise he was dead.

FIFTY-TWO
REVISITING A DEAD-END JOB

DAVY VOLUNTEERED to make the coffin. Apparently, he had once worked as an apprentice for a coastal undertaker.

'I never knew that?' Hendrik said when the deckhand volunteered this over a cup of tea in the kitchen.

'Why would I tell anyone?' Davy said. 'It was hardly a highlight of my working life. I was straight out of high school, and that was the only job going.'

'I didn't even know you finished high school?' Hendrik said.

'Never said I did. The headmaster called me into his office when I was near the end of grade nine. I held out my hand like I normally did but he said I wasn't in trouble this time. I remember clear as day what he said. "I think we've come to the limit of what we can teach you." I was confused. What was he saying? That I was too clever? That I should skip grade 10, 11 and 12 and go straight to university? Turns out, he was asking me to leave at the end of the year.'

'So you finished the apprenticeship?' Hendrik said.

'I didn't say that either. Making the coffins was OK, I suppose. I got used to the embalming too. But I couldn't handle all that crying, all those mournful people at the graveside. Funerals are so depressing.'

'Well, you don't have to worry this time,' Hendrik said. 'I don't think there'll be a lot of crying at Darkey's funeral.'

Davy smiled. 'Tell you another thing I never liked? Digging the hole.'

He looked from Hendrik to Ralph. 'But I'm guessing that's what you two blokes will be doing while I'm making the coffin.'

FIFTY-THREE
DIG IT

THEY FOUND two shovels in the basement. That place was an amazing resource. Davy even found enough timber from the remaining crates to make the coffin.

Hendrik was all for locking Darkey's body in the basement, throwing away the key, and using the saved time to look for the beacon so he could turn it back on.

'That's what he would have wanted,' he reasoned. 'Do you really think him and Whitey planned to bury *us* after they shot us?'

'Maybe not,' Ralph said. 'But we have to rise above the likes of them. There will be plenty of time to look for the beacon after we do the decent thing.'

Besides, Mad Bill had told Ralph how much he was looking forward to this funeral. The old man was treating it as a dress rehearsal for his own sending-off. 'I never expected someone else to go before me, so this will give me a chance to iron out the kinks.'

Mad Bill said he didn't mind if none of the others could actually dress up for the funeral. He, however, planned to dress in the island's one-and-only suit for the occasion. But he insisted that suit wouldn't be visible at his own funeral because he'd be wearing it inside the closed coffin he had requested.

The first hurdle Hendrik and Ralph had was finding a position for the grave.

Mad Bill had already picked out his own preferred spot, in the shade of a frangipani tree.

So, under his supervision, they opted for a spot on the other side of the existing graves.

Hendrik found it tough digging in bare feet.

An hour in, they hit something hard.

Mad Bill said he'd go fetch the crowbar from the basement so they could shift the obstruction. Hendrik and Ralph were very pleased he had such a thing, and while he was gone they took a well-earned breather, sitting on the side with their legs dangling into the hole, speculating that perhaps they had hit the coral reef, in which case the crowbar would be useless anyway. Maybe this was as low as they were going to go?

When Mad Bill returned with the crowbar, they used it to reveal the obstacle, which surprisingly turned out to be a solid barrier of mortar and bricks.

That didn't make any sense — until Hendrik put some grunt into the crowbar.

With a crack and a rumble, a gaping hole opened up beneath and they looked down into the tunnel below.

Hendrik saw them coming first. 'Rats! Get out, get out.'

Ralph climbed out of the grave just in time. Dozens and dozens of rats scrambled up the sides of the grave and scurried towards the undergrowth.

'Get them,' Mad Bill cried. 'Hit them with your shovels. We need more candles.'

FIFTY-FOUR
DEAD BUGGERS CAN'T BE CHOOSERS

THEY HAD no choice but to start digging a new grave.

Mad Bill refused to give up his chosen final resting place, so they settled on a spot just behind the bench.

It seemed like an odd spot to Ralph, but Hendrik pointed out that at least it was away from the alignment of the tunnel. And Mad Bill added his deciding vote.

'The bugger has to take where he can get,' Mad Bill said. 'Ordinarily I'd agree to bung him in the basement but I plan to move my sherry back down there and I don't want to have to see his decaying corpse every time I feel like a tipple.'

'You're all heart,' Ralph said.

'He's just lucky he was such a good mailman, who built up some brownie points.'

So they dug the new hole.

Hendrik complained all the way of blisters on his hands and feet. Mad Bill was no help.

Nor was Davy, who had by now finished making the coffin. The sensible thing would have been to take the coffin up to where Darkey's body was. But that had never occurred to Davy. Instead, he rolled the corpse down to the basement, using gravity to bump, bump, bump down two flights of stairs.

'You should have asked one of us to help you?' Ralph said, when he came outside puffing and sweating, and holding a glass of water.

'I knew you blokes were busy,' He sat down on the ground next to Mad Bill.

Hendrik scowled at him. 'What do you think you're doing?'

'I didn't ask you to help *me*,' Davy said.

'Have you forgotten who pays your wages?'

'Now you don't actually have a boat, I figured I was unemployed again.'

Davy took a sip of his water. 'I'm looking forward to this. Who knew grave digging was a spectator sport?'

FIFTY-FIVE
KEEPER OF LOST SOLES

THE FIRST SURPRISE they had was when they laid eyes on the coffin the next morning.

Darkey's bare feet were sticking out of a hole at one end.

Davy shrugged. 'Measuring up was never my strong point, probably why they let me go. Good thing I found a keyhole saw in the basement though, eh?'

Then he realised they were looking down at his newly acquired footwear with looks of astonishment.

'What? Darkey didn't need them any more.'

Hendrik frowned. 'Have you no shame?'

Davy shrugged again. 'It's one of the perks of the job. You're just jealous you didn't lay your hands on them first!'

'At least they would have fitted me better than you. What are they? Three sizes too big?'

They excused Mad Bill from pall-bearing duties. At his height and weight, he wouldn't have been any help carrying the coffin, especially up the flight of stairs from the basement, which was hard yakka in the narrow stairwell.

He was wearing a top hat when he came down the stairs and slipped in behind them as they headed for the front door.

The suit looked four sizes too big but perhaps it had been the height of fashion in 1943. Someone had left it behind in a wardrobe.

'Remember, you need to treat this as a dress rehearsal,' Mad Bill said. 'Pretend I'm not here, just like I won't be then.'

This was easier said than done. He walked behind them most of the way to the graveyard, shouting instructions like a coxswain. 'Left a bit, left, right, faster, careful now, you don't want to drop him.'

Darkey was heavy. Hendrik and Ralph had either side of the front of the coffin (actually the protruding feet indicated it was really the back end, so the coffin was back to front) and poor Davy had the other end, which they told him would be the light end on account of Darkey's empty head.

When they were nearly there, Mad Bill scooted around them and knelt on the bench so he could see them set the coffin down.

When he saw the feet sticking out, he made the sign of the cross.

'I'll be right back.' He rushed towards the house.

The others were actually glad of the unscheduled break in the program because it gave them the chance to catch their breath and regain their composure. But they looked at each other blankly because they didn't have a clue what was going on.

When Mad Bill returned, he was carrying a set of hedge clippers. 'These were the only things I could find at short notice. We can't bury him like that! Just look at the length of his toenails.'

Mad Bill knelt down and went to work with his pedicure. Darkey was lucky he was dead, otherwise he might have felt some pain.

'You know that's a waste of time.' Davy watched him chop. 'Toenails keep growing when you're dead and buried.'

'How do you know that?' Mad Bill raised a hand, hoping someone would help him up.

'It's well known in the funeral business.'

Ralph helped Mad Bill up and the old man brushed the dirt from his knees. 'Well, all the more reason to trim fingernails and toenails before you return someone to the earth. Just remember that when it's my turn. I've got some proper clippers around the house somewhere. Remind me to look for them.'

He looked down at the huge clippers. 'I don't want you using these things on me. I don't even know why we have these on the island. It's not like we even have hedges.'

Mad Bill's eyes focused on the coffin.

'Someone should say a few words.' The old man looked up at Hendrik.

Hendrik raised his palms defensively. 'Oh no, not me. I'm still angry at him for hiding the emergency beacon.'

Mad Bill switched his focus to Ralph.

'I hardly knew him — except when he clearly wasn't at his best.'

Mad Bill rolled his eyes, and turned to Davy. 'You must have had some experience at this kind of thing, sonny.'

'Not really. But I'll have a go, if you like.'

He bowed his head and put his hand on his heart. The other three of them followed his lead.

'Almighty,' Davy said. 'Shit happens, Lord.'

He paused.

What he then said shocked them even more. 'Zombie!' he cried.

FIFTY-SIX

BACK FROM THE DEAD

TWO DIRTY HANDS had appeared over the side of the abandoned grave.

Then a familiar head appeared. It was eye-less, one-eared and covered in bites and blood.

But it was clearly Whitey. His long, straggly hair made him look even more ghoulish.

'Help me,' he groaned, as he climbed out of the grave.

But he was beyond help. They could see that. It's a good thing he keeled over and died right there.

Right after Hendrik removed his shoes, Davy, who now had some experience in rolling cadavers, pushed him straight back into the hole. They quickly filled the grave with dirt before Whitey had the chance to come back alive.

They gave Darkey a more respectful send-off.

As they lowered the coffin into the grave, they all sang *Will The Circle Be Unbroken*, which is the song Mad Bill had stipulated in his new will and wanted them to practise. Ralph could tell from the look on the old man's face he wasn't impressed.

Hendrik got over himself and did say a few words.

Ralph hadn't seen him so choked up.

'You big, stupid oaf,' he said as he threw the first sod into the open grave. 'I remember the first day you came to work for me.'

'Best mailman I ever had,' Mad Bill said.

'Thanks for the shoes,' Davy said.

FIFTY-SEVEN
A MAN'S GOTTA HAVE SOME VICES

HENDRIK WATCHED with disgust as Mad Bill shovelled another spoonful of Rice Bubbles into his mouth.

'How can you eat at a time like this?'

'Wiiggemyyaga,yoni,oullunersad. Ouneffwxrnooqwe-nilleourasteat,' Mad Bill said.

'I can't understand a word you are saying, you stupid old goat.'

Mad Bill swallowed. 'I said: when you get to my age, sonny, you'll understand. It's not healthy to die on an empty stomach.'

They were sitting around the table in the kitchen downstairs. Mad Bill had placed a variety pack of cereal boxes on the table, along with cartons of long-life milk and bowls and spoons. 'Help your-selves,' he had said, but they hadn't and he was now Rice Bubbling solo. 'Suit yourselves. That just means there'll be more here for my wake. You'll have to eat them then, you know? I've written it into my new will.'

'You don't get it, do you?' Hendrik said. 'As soon as we find that emergency beacon and turn it back on, help will be on its way. You might choose to stay on the island, but the rest of us will be out of here.'

The old man swallowed and fixed his gaze firmly on the skipper.

'Aren't you interested in hanging around long enough to retrieve the gold from the tunnel?'

'And risk being chewed up by rats!'

'They've probably all escaped to the surface. Even the rats couldn't wait to leave that tunnel.'

'Maybe, but I'm not in a hurry to find out.'

'Aren't you curious about whether or not the tunnels go to the mainland?'

'Why should I be? Once we find the beacon, they'll send a boat or chopper to rescue us.'

Mad Bill chewed thoughtfully. They could tell he was about to say something.

'What if I told you I had already found this beacon thing?' he said.

'What?' Ralph said.

'Where?' Davy said.

'When?' Hendrik said.

'Not long before Darkey's funeral,' Mad Bill said. 'I found it in the place I keep my hats.'

'You mean you have other hats?' Ralph said.

'A man's got to have some vices.'

'You've got extra quotas, you silly old goat,' Hendrik said. 'Where is this blasted hat cupboard?'

Mad Bill picked up his bowl, lifted it to his lips and slurped down the remaining milk, before slamming it back down.

'It's my secret hiding place. If I told you, I'd have to kill you, or you'd have to kill me. And if you go to all that trouble, when you open my will you'll find that you're going to have to bury me.'

A loud noise outside drowned out the simmering silence.

Ralph went to the window and saw a grey helicopter touch down next to the vegetable garden with a whoosh-whoosh-whoosh.

He could hear Hendrik and Davy's excitement behind him. They had seen what Ralph had seen and it sounded like they were doing some kind of jig.

With its rotor blades slowing down, the helicopter door opened and a man in a flying suit headed for the front door.

FIFTY-EIGHT
I'VE ALREADY GOT SOME

MAD BILL TURNED for the door. 'This used to be a quiet island!'

The three others followed right behind him, and he turned on them. 'Where'd you think you young blokes are going?' he hissed.

Hendrik's eyes widened. 'I reckon it's us he wants, not you.'

'It's *my* house,' Mad Bill said.

'And it's your decision if you want to stay here. But the rest of us just want to go home. Ralph especially.'

They arrived en masse at the front door, only to see Mad Bill had deadlocked it.

The noise of the rotor-blade had almost stopped and they heard the man's knock clearly, but Mad Bill made no attempt to retrieve the key from wherever he had put it.

He yelled through the door. 'If you're trying to sell me encyclopaedias, sonny, I've already got some.'

The initial answer was the sound of sniggering. Clearly, there was more than one person on the other side. 'We're from the Royal Australian Navy, sir.'

'Don't give me that! You arrived in a helicopter, not a ship. We saw you out the window.'

Ralph lowered his voice to Mad Bill. 'Actually, the Navy does have helicopters, not just ships and submarines.'

Mad Bill bristled. 'See, that's what I mean about this country going to ruin. The Navy should stick to its core business. Things that float. Now they're flying from door to door trying to sell stuff.'

He turned again and shouted at the door. 'Go away. I don't want to buy a helicopter.'

A new voice replied. It was a woman's voice. 'We're not trying to sell you anything, sir. We're looking for a gentleman named William Clarin.'

Mad Bill looked back at Ralph, puzzled. 'I thought you said they were Navy? That sounds like sheila's voice!'

'They have lots of women in the Navy these days,' Ralph said.

Mad Bill's face went white.

If the three other men hadn't picked this moment to shout all at once, the Navy people might have been able to understand they needed help.

But when their din stopped, the woman spoke. 'The gentleman we're looking for is supposed to be a hermit. I can hear you have company. Sorry to have troubled you, sir.'

Their footsteps faded as they clip-clopped down the steps.

The three men desperate to leave went to the window in the kitchen, only to find that was locked too. They probably should have broken the glass to catch attention. Instead, they all waved their hands, jumped up and down, and shouted. But any noise they made was drowned out by the helicopter roaring into life. They watched as it lifted into the sky and then disappeared into the west until the speck on the horizon disappeared.

FIFTY-NINE
WILLIAM CLARIN STANDS UP

WHEN THEY FINALLY TURNED AROUND, they saw that Mad Bill had already resumed his seat at the kitchen table.

'I guess that means you young bucks will be staying on. Any ideas how we're going to get the shotgun back? I have to hunt if we want to eat.'

Hendrik almost had steam coming out his ears. 'You ought to have thought of that. If you had opened the door, we could have all been rescued. You'd never have to eat snake again!'

Hendrik turned a chair around backwards and straddled it. Ralph could tell Mad Bill didn't approve, which is why he and Davy sat back down in the seats exactly how they had left them.

'I never stopped you from opening the door,' Mad Bill said. '*I* just didn't want to. Not without my shotgun! Just because they knew who I was, doesn't mean I felt I could trust them.'

'They knew you?' Hendrik's eyes narrowed.

'They knew my name, didn't they?'

'You're William Clarin? Why didn't you say so!'

The old man shrugged. 'Everyone's called me Mad Bill since I arrived on this island in 1974.'

'Why were they even looking for you?' Hendrik's eyes bulged. 'Are you on some kind of a wanted list?'

'Not that I know of.'

'It never occurred to you to open the door and identify yourself.'

'Why didn't you open it if you were so curious?'

'I didn't have the fucking key.'

'Didn't you see it lying on the ledge there next to the door?'

'No.'

'I keep all my keys on ledges next to doors and windows. You can't lose them that way.'

Ralph looked across to the kitchen window. Sure enough, the key was right there.

SIXTY

WE JUST WANT TO GO HOME

HENDRIK GLARED AT MAD BILL. 'Sitting around isn't helping us find that emergency beacon. You can save us time by showing us your hat cupboard.'

The old man held his withering gaze. 'It's my business where I hide my hats, sonny.'

'I couldn't care less about your hats.' Hendrik threw his hands in the air as he stood up and the chair scraped on the floor. 'I just don't get it. Maybe you *are* on a wanted list, which is why you want to stay put. But: We. Just. Don't. Care. I can't believe you sabotaged our best chance to go home!'

'Nothing I can do about it now.' Mad Bill's puny shoulders shrugged. 'Guess you'll just have to help me get my shotgun and gold back.'

'I have no intention of putting my life on the line.'

'Even for half the gold bars?'

'Half?' Hendrik slowly sat again.

'That's what I said, didn't I?'

Davy put his hand up, like he was back in school and the others all looked at him, which he took as permission to speak. 'If I help, can I have half too?'

Hendrik closed his eyes. 'Dipshit! If you get half, and I get half, that leaves nothing for Mad Bill.'

'I didn't invite you, sonny, just in case we run across Whitey's body again,' Mad Bill said to Davy. 'Last thing I'd want is you getting all hysterical thinking you'd seen another zombie. But I'll tell you what. If the rats get Hendrik you can be up next.'

Mad Bill eyes fell on Ralph. 'Sorry, sonny, but I don't think you'd be cut out for this either.'

Ralph raised his palms. 'I'm fine with that. If by some miracle I get home in time to see my daughter being born, I'd really prefer not to have a face full of rat bites when she looks up into my eyes that first time.'

Ralph looked across at Hendrik. 'You've changed your tune in a hurry!'

The skipper stroked his facial hair. It was getting to five days' growth now. 'It just occurred to me: what's the hurry? The missus doesn't want to see me home till Christmas anyway. And a bit of gold wouldn't go astray.'

Ralph said: 'But you won't mind if I go looking for the hat cupboard while you're away in the tunnel?'

Mad Bill started cackling, which Ralph found odd because he didn't think what he said was all that funny.

'Darkey *did* find it but I don't think he's likely to blab, do you?' the old man snorted. 'But even if you manage to contact him in a seance, it won't do you any good. The beacon isn't in my hat cupboard any more. I took it out and hid it elsewhere.'

SIXTY-ONE
IF I SAY RUN, RUUUUNNN

THE FOUR OF them stood at the entrance to the tunnel. 'You look worried, sonny?' Mad Bill said.

'Of course I'm worried.' Hendrik wiped his brow with a handker-chief. 'We don't know for sure all the rats have left the tunnel.'

'Relax.' Mad Bill tapped the side of the candle he was holding on a little tray. 'The stinky candles have never let me down.'

'But what if it goes out?'

Mad Bill held up a box of matches and shook it under Hendrik's nose. 'I'll just relight it.'

Hendrik considered this, then said: 'Where'd you get all these matches anyway?'

'Paid one of my gold bars for them. I have a whole cupboard full of them upstairs.'

Hendrik sighed. 'Those door-to-door salesmen must all have seen you coming? They're probably buying each other expensive drinks in a Pacific resort right now and laughing at you.'

'Why do you say that?'

'Well, you don't think a gold bar is a bit over the odds for even a large supply of matches?'

'Needs must. Have you ever tried rubbing two sticks together to make fire when a battalion of rats is rapidly heading towards you? If the salesman had pushed harder I would have been happy to part with two or three more gold bars for all them matches. Let me ask you this? If it had been in your power, how many gold bars would you have been willing to pay for that helicopter?'

'That's different. I would have offered them every last bit of gold.' Even in the flickering glow of the basement, Ralph could see the pained look on Hendrik's face.

Mad Bill shrugged. 'That's the problem with your generation! Spend, spend, spend. Money doesn't grow on trees, you know! Good thing you don't even own half the gold bars yet.'

Hendrik sucked in a deep breath. 'That's why I'm here though.'

'I suppose you think that helicopter's coming back?'

'I can only hope.'

'It won't do you any good to have *half* the gold bars when you need to buy *all* the helicopter.'

'I'm sure you'd find it in your cold, old heart to help.'

'Why would I help you? I don't even know that you can drive a helicopter.'

'I wouldn't have to. For all that gold, I'm sure she'd fly us to wherever we wanted.'

'*She*? You're not serious? The Navy wouldn't let a woman fly that thing!'

'I saw her get into the driver's side.'

'See what the world's coming to! Back in the day, she'd be pushing the tea trolley up the aisle and she would have been happy to do it.'

'You'd have no choice but to trust her,' Hendrik said. 'If I was trying to fly that whirly-bird you wouldn't end up anywhere but still here. I've driven all kinds of boats, I've driven a few tow-trucks but I've never even been in a helicopter…'

'I'd rather take my chances with you than her. Even if she can get that thing off the ground without kangaroo hops, that Navy girlie could be a spy. Everyone could end up in Russia.'

Hendrik pointed to the candle. 'So you're sure that will protect us?'

Mad Bill shrugged. 'In theory, yes. But we might be dealing with a breed of rats that have evolved completely underground.'

'What are you saying?'

Mad Bill set his jaw. 'If I say run, ruuuunnn.'

SIXTY-TWO
TWO HUMAN POPSICLES INSIDE A YELLOW RAFT

RALPH AND DAVY watched the light of the candle fade as Mad Bill and Hendrik crept into the tunnel.

'This isn't helping us get home,' Davy said.

'I dunno,' Ralph said. 'If the candles really do protect them from rats perhaps the tunnels are our way to the mainland.'

'I guess we'll soon find out.' Davy squinted. 'Looks like they're just going round the bend now.'

'Listen out then,' Ralph said. 'Remember, Mad Bill anointed you first reserve.'

Davy glanced sideways. He didn't look happy.

'Ain't no way I'm going into this tunnel if I hear screams. Truth is I've never been that fond of the skipper. And Mad Bill has already had a good innings.'

'You were all keen before — when you thought you might get a share of the gold.'

Davy put his finger to his lips. 'Shhhh.' He looked hard down the tunnel. 'You hear that?'

Ralph cocked his ear. 'I can't hear anything.'

'Exactly. Shouldn't we be hearing something? Screams? Voices? The hissing of rats? Something?'

'Sound doesn't travel that well around corners,' Ralph said. 'They're probably trying to fix the wheels back on the trolley.'

'What's taking them so long?' Davy said. 'If they don't come out, you'll be relying on me to work out how we're going to get off this island.'

'You? God help us!'

'Why do you say that? As it happens, I already have the beginnings of a plan.'

'Sure you have! Don't tell me you're planning to build your own helicopter out of packing boxes!'

'Are you taking the piss? What I have in mind is we take that life-raft from upstairs, see, and pull it back to the water. All we have to do is paddle out to that current where I was saved by those ducks and, bingo, let Mother Nature take its course.'

'Didn't Mad Bill say that current travels down to the Antarctic?' Ralph said. 'They'd probably two human popsicles inside a yellow raft.'

Davy's voice rose: 'Do you have a better idea?'

'Well, when Santa Claus visits with our presents we could pop out from behind the chimney and hijack his sleigh.'

Davy studied Ralph's face. 'Really? He comes here?'

Ralph didn't have the chance to answer him.

They heard noises in the tunnel before they saw Mad Bill and Hendrik come around the bend.

'I'm pulling as hard as I can. It would help if you got off and pushed.' Hendrik had a rope tied around his waist and was pulling the trolley towards the entrance.

Mad Bill was atop the trolley. He waved his shotgun triumphantly. 'Tonight we celebrate. No snake is safe from the dinner pot!'

SIXTY-THREE
THE GHOST OF CHRISTMAS PASTA

IF YOU EVER FIND YOURSELF in a position where you simply must eat snake, it helps greatly to be able to wash it down with 80-year-old sherry.

Mad Bill and Hendrik were both in excellent moods, having retrieved the gold and the shotgun. Now that Hendrik was resigned to not getting off the island just yet, he seemed so much more relaxed.

When Ralph told him about Davy's plan to use the life-raft to escape, he just scoffed.

'That's a terrible plan,' he said.

'That's what I told him.'

Davy kept chomping on the other side of the table, pretending he couldn't even hear their conversation.

'I don't know why you don't just go through the tunnel?' Hendrik said. 'That's what I plan to do just before Christmas. I can't wait to see the expression on Madge's face when I come through that door carrying two crayfish and pulling all that gold.'

Davy suddenly chipped in. 'She'll probably think you're a ghost?'

'I'm counting on it. The ghost of Christmas pasta.'

Davy picked some snake scales out from between his teeth. 'Let's hope she hasn't remarried by then.'

Hendrik gave him the death stare.

'Wouldn't surprise me if they reckon all three of us were lost at sea,' Davy said. 'Probably too early to hold memorial services, but they'll come in the next few weeks. I can't see Madge being a widow too long, can you skipper? Good cook like her?'

Hendrik's face lost its sunny disposition. He opened his mouth to speak but nothing came out.

Ralph filled the silence. 'All the more reason for me to get home. I don't want to put Maria through all that angst of a memorial service.'

Davy weighed in again. 'Yes, it's even worse for you. Being young and fertile, she'll probably be a widow for less time than fat old Madge.'

Hendrik half stood up. 'How would you like me to come over there and punch you?'

Ralph dragged him back down to his seat. 'He's just trying to wind us up, Hendrik. Payback for us ridiculing his life-raft escape plan.'

'I told you,' Davy said. 'I'm not going into that tunnel. I'm the youngest one here, so I've got more life expectancy to lose.'

Ralph studied his face. 'Are you younger than me? I'm 31.'

'I'm 32, but I haven't got a kid on the way. That makes me younger in kid years.'

Ralph looked back to Hendrik, who shrugged.

'Second thoughts,' Hendrik said, 'maybe there is merit in the life-raft plan. I'm fine with escaping through the tunnel just before Christmas but if you two fellows want to be rescued earlier, Davy's life-raft plan might just work for you.'

'How?'

'Easy. We set off the emergency beacon and tether it to the raft so the search planes will find you.'

'And that'll work?' Ralph said.

'Can't see why not? All we have to do is find where old Bugalugs has hidden it.'

All eyes fell on Mad Bill, and it wasn't because he had now lifted his empty plate to his lips and was licking the last of the white gravy.

When he put the plate down, he realised there was no way to avoid the conversation.

'I don't know what the hurry is about,' he said. 'Christmas is always such a lovely time on the island. I thought you blokes would want to stick around and help me decorate the trees.'

'There's not one pine tree on this island,' Davy said.

'That's where you're wrong. I've got a bunch of artificial Christmas trees.'

'Let me guess?' Hendrik said. 'You paid a gold ingot for them?'

'What do you take me for?' Mad Bill said. 'A cheapskate? I paid one gold bar for *each* of the six trees. And I threw in another one just because I was feeling all Christmasy.'

'Christ!' Hendrik said. 'How many bars were here when you came?'

'Let's not get sidetracked over this,' Ralph said. 'I know, Hendrik, you're OK about staying on for a while, but Davy and I want to get home as soon as possible.'

'No way am I risking that tunnel, even with shoes,' Davy said again.

Ralph scowled at him. 'I think we've established that. What we're talking about now is Hendrik's amendment to your plan.'

Hendrik looked across to Mad Bill. 'Unless you tell us where you've hidden the beacon, we're back at square one.'

The old man smiled mischievously, then rubbed his hands together. 'I can feel a treasure hunt coming on. Won't that be fun? If you find this thing you're looking for, you can keep it. I can't be fairer than that!'

He uncorked the bottle in the middle of the table and reached over to top up all the empty glasses.

He then surveyed the three plates of stew, which hadn't been finished. 'Come on, eat up. This is a special treat. Normally, the snakes I cook have fed on the plumpest rats on the island but my guess is the snakes I shot today had dined on rats that had got plump by dining on Whitey.'

SIXTY-FOUR
I'VE JUST GOTTA GET A MESSAGE TO YOU

MAD BILL WAS keen to do the treasure hunt straight after dinner but the other three persuaded him it would be better to do it in the morning when they had clear heads.

'Please yourself,' he said. 'I'll get in an early night too. I have to rat-proof this house again tomorrow. I mightn't even have time for the treasure hunt.'

'Does that mean you'll just tell us where the beacon is?' Hendrik said.

'Nice try, sonny,' Mad Bill put both hands on the table to leverage himself up. 'I'll just have to make time.'

They heard his footsteps disappearing up the stairs.

The others followed shortly after.

It was Ralph's fifth night away from Maria. They wouldn't really have held his memorial service, would they? If only he could get a message to her and tell her he was all right?

SIXTY-FIVE
DO YOU GIVE UP?

RALPH COULDN'T REMEMBER the last time he had participated in a treasure hunt, especially straight after his Rice Bubbles.

But the rules came flooding back to him when Mad Bill flitted between the three visitors, jumping up and down like an excited child and telling them they were either cold or very cold or warmer.

The old house had a lot of hiding places, just as he had said. Who had the British wanted to hide stuff from?

They found the hat cupboard. Mad Bill wouldn't have been able to reach it without a step ladder, but Hendrik had no trouble.

'Aha, what have we got here?' he said.

This wiped the smile off Mad Bill's face.

'My hat cupboard is private,' he snarled. 'I told you: I've relocated what you're looking for.'

'Yes, but how do we know you really did? We need to make sure you're not doing a double bluff.'

Mad Bill put his hand on his heart. 'I'm very honest. Ask the people who voted for me?'

'You didn't even vote for yourself, you silly old goat!'

'That's not fair! Even if I had wanted to go against my beliefs and vote, I had no way of getting to the polling booth, did I?'

'And I've got no way of knowing if you're telling the truth unless I empty this cupboard.'

You've seen magicians pull rabbits out of hats? Well, pulling hats out of the cupboard had the same kind of theatre.

Out came the top hat. They already knew about that but it didn't stop Mad Bill repeatedly jumping up with outstretched arms like he was a frustrated short-arse on a basketball team. Hendrik thought the hat would look nice on his own head, which just made Mad Bill jump more trying to retrieve it.

Hendrik fended him off with one hand, and used the other to pull out the next hat.

It was a cap. Hendrik examined the embroidered letters. They said MAKE AUSTRALIA GRATE AGAIN.

'Leave my election cap alone.' Mad Bill had slumped into a chair in the hallway, red-faced from his exertions. 'That cost me two gold bars to have done, that did.'

Hendrik threw it to the floor.

Next hat out of the cache was a green shower hat, which was a real mystery.

Then came a Santa hat.

Hendrik held it by the tip. 'You don't actually wear this?'

Mad Bill put out his bottom lip. 'Not that one, no,' he mumbled.

Some clarity came when Hendrik reached in and pulled out three more Santa hats. 'What the …?'

Mad Bill shrugged. 'You just never know when you'll have guests for Christmas.' He exhaled and took another deep breath before he continued. 'Just as well Whitey and Darkey aren't still alive, eh? I wouldn't have enough hats to go around.'

'You don't get it, do you?' Hendrik threw the Santa hats back into the cupboard and pointed from Ralph to Davy. 'These guys want to go *now*.'

Mad Bill had recovered from his exertions, and began cackling. 'Not if you can't find my new hiding place, they're not.'

Ralph thought Hendrik was going to pick the old man up by the suspenders again but he showed remarkable restraint.

He put his hands on his hips. 'How many gold bars did you pay for those hats?'

'It's all about money with you, isn't it? Bah humbug. I'm glad you're not staying till Christmas. You'd just spoil it.'

The treasure hunt resumed.

They looked under beds, on top of wardrobes, they rifled through every drawer and cupboard visible in the house. Hendrik thought he had hit the jackpot when he discovered the secret compartment at the back of the cupboard under the stairwell, which only opened when the vertical part of the third step was pushed in. But all the space yielded were the six artificial Christmas trees covered in spider webs.

'Do you give up?' Mad Bill was the only one who still had any kind of gleam in his eyes.

'Yes, we give up.' Even without checking with the others, Ralph knew by their long faces he could speak for them.

'If I tell you, we have to make a deal. You get nothing for nothing in this house.'

What he wanted first was one of Hendrik's gold bars, but that didn't go down well at all with the skipper, who said he didn't care about Davy and Ralph *that* much.

What ensued was a silly compromise.

SIXTY-SIX
FESTIVE GOLD-PAINTED COCONUTS

THEY DECIDED to skip lunch and sit on the grass next to the vegetable patch to fulfil their end of the bargain.

Ralph didn't know how the others felt about wearing Santa hats while they worked but he knew he felt silly.

He had never tried to paint a coconut before. It was just as well there was so much paint in the basement.

'I wonder why they left some much gold paint behind?' Davy said.

'Beats me,' Mad Bill said. 'Many a year I've wished for a bit more variety, even just silver.'

The bell on the tip of Hendrik's hat jingled. 'So you've used coconuts as baubles before?'

'I had no choice. The salesman who sold me the trees promised me he'd be back the next year with some decorations but he never returned. I don't know why. He probably went to jail too.'

'Aren't coconuts a bit too big to hang on little Christmas trees?'

'Course they are,' Mad Bill said. 'They look bloody silly. But luckily no-one has ever complained.'

Hendrik dipped his brush in the can and slapped it on the side to remove the excess paint. His hat had the only bell, which is how come he was the only one who tinkled. He dabbed at his coconut again.

'Remind me not to have a nap under a Christmas tree, fellas. Wouldn't want one of these to fall on your moosh!'

They sat there quietly working. When Ralph realised he was away with the fairies, he just knew this paint had some old-time mind-altering chemicals.

'Why would the military leave gold paint anyway? I thought they only did khaki and grey,' Davy said.

'My theory,' Mad Bill said, 'is the medical isolation people left all the gold paint. Who knows why the military left all those iron bars?'

If Hendrik was stoned like the rest of them, he sure snapped out of it in a hurry. He jingle-jangled furiously and his face took on the colours of Christmas: it went green, then white, then red. 'W-what?' He pointed a trembling finger at Mad Bill. 'What did you say?'

Mad Bill, who was sitting cross-legged on the ground, cackled. 'You didn't think they were real gold, did you?'

SIXTY-SEVEN
'I'M DREAMING OF A WHITEY CHRISTMAS.'

THIS TIME HENDRIK did pick Mad Bill up by the suspenders. One minute the old man was sitting on the ground, the next he was swinging around in the air.

'Do you think that's why the Christmas tree salesman never came back?' Hendrik's eyes were wild, his bell was going hell for leather, and Mad Bill was getting one heck of a wedgie. 'You're the one who should be in jail. What do you reckon the Christmas tree salesman thought when he scraped off the paint and realised he had been duped?'

Davy and Ralph leapt up. 'Put him down,' Ralph said. 'We don't want anyone else to get hurt.'

Hendrik did put him down, but as soon as he released him, he balled up his fists. Davy held him the skipper back.

'What's the problem?' Mad Bill adjusted his clothing. 'I never claimed they were anything other than gold bars. It wasn't my fault if you thought they were 24-carat bars.'

Hendrik shook his head. The noise he made was definitely more jangle than jingle now. 'I can't believe you let me risk my life by going into that tunnel!'

'You were the one who was greedy for the gold? I really just wanted my shotgun. We've got to eat. And you never know who might come around?'

Hendrik was shouting now. 'Not the Christmas tree man, that's for sure! The encyclopaedia man? The hat man? The cereal man? Anyone else you've fooled?'

'Darkey and Whitey.'

'I feel sorry for those two silly buggers now. All the time they thought they were ripping you off! Turns out it was the other way round! You killed them.'

'Serves them right then. I've always said cheats never prosper.'

Hendrik gritted his teeth. True to his word, he helped distribute the trees around the island, and hang the gold-*painted* coconuts from them. But you could see he wasn't happy.

'You'd better keep up your side of the bargain, you old goat.' He waved a finger at Mad Bill. 'I want you to go fetch that emergency beacon right now.'

'I've never reneged on a deal in my life, sonny.' Mad Bill pointed to the graveyard. 'That tree goes over there, so we can brighten the place up. He croaked out a bit of a song. "I'm dreaming of a Whitey Christmas."'

SIXTY-EIGHT
BRINGING HOME THE BEACON

TWENTY MINUTES HAD PASSED and Mad Bill hadn't returned. The three of them were sitting on the park bench, like three Christmas elves in a graveyard adorned with golden coconuts.

'Where do you think he is?' Davy turned his head, with a swish of his Santa hat. He was on one end of the bench and Ralph was on the other end.

'Dunno,' the man in the middle said. Hendrik's hat tinkled as he spoke. 'I knew we should have gone with him though.'

'Relax,' Ralph said. 'It's not like he has anywhere else to go.'

'What's the bet he's forgotten where he's hidden it?' Hendrik said.

Davy's eyes opened wide. 'Maybe he's escaped into the tunnel?'

'Why would he do that?' Ralph said. 'He doesn't even want to leave this crumby island.'

'No, but he might be running in fear of his life?' Davy looked accusingly at Hendrik.

'Don't look at me like that! I just wanted to shake some sense into him.'

'Shhh,' Ralph said. 'Here he comes.'

Mad Bill was walking towards them carrying something yellow in his right hand.

'Sorry I was so long,' Mad Bill said when he came within earshot. 'I had to wash it. It took some scrubbing too.'

Hendrik was wearing the biggest smile he had had all day. 'It wouldn't have mattered to me if it had been a bit grubby.'

'Trust me, it would have mattered.' Mad Bill handed the beacon to the skipper, who raised it to his lips and kissed it.

Ralph could see Mad Bill cringe.

'What?' Hendrik said.

'Nothing! What you don't know can't hurt you.'

SIXTY-NINE
SUBMERGED TREASURE

HENDRIK LOOKED PERPLEXED after he flicked the switch on the side of the beacon. Ralph didn't know if it was supposed to go beep, beep, beep or start flashing, but he had expected it to do something and Hendrik obviously did too.

Hendrik held the beacon up to his ear and called for shush.

'I don't understand it,' he said. 'Darkey said it was working fine before he switched it off.'

'You don't think the sherry did leak into it,' Ralph said.

'It's waterproof.' Hendrik said. 'It's designed to float.'

'That's a mighty relief to hear,' Mad Bill said.

Hendrik looked up at him. 'Are you trying to tell me you hid it somewhere wet?'

Mad Bill looked from one end of the bench to the other. 'I'm not saying.'

'What's it matter now the treasure hunt game is over?' Ralph said.

Mad Bill waggled a finger. '*That* game might be over, sonny, but I haven't given up on you youngsters playing again. So I'm not about to reveal one of my best hiding places.'

Davy jumped up from the bench. 'So what are we going to do now?'

Hendrik looked down at the beacon in his hands. 'I'm sure I'll be able to fix it.'

'Since when have you fixed anything, skipper?'

'I fixed up that old radio, didn't I?'

'The one Darkey smashed up before you had the chance to confess it didn't actually work? Admit it. You're all talk. No wonder *The Good Lady* sank!'

'It sank because those bozos weren't looking where they were going.'

'Nothing to do with your neglect of maintenance over the years then?'

'What are you talking about?' Now Hendrik stood and looked down on his deckhand. They would have been face to face, except for the height differential. So it was more nose to forehead. 'How can you say that? That boat was state of the art.'

'Shit, that boat was older than you are!' Davy said.

'So what? The life-raft is older than you are but it got Whitey and Darkey to the island just fine, didn't it?'

Davy's Adam's apple bobbed. 'That raft is thirty-two years old?'

'At least.'

'But I remember when you bought it. It looked shiny and new 10 years ago.'

'The previous owner had really looked after it.' Hendrik lifted the beacon to Davy's eye-line. 'Same with this, which came as part of the package.'

The blood drained from Davy's face. 'You mean that's 32 years old too?'

Hendrik shrugged. 'No way of telling! But if it is that old that's not necessarily a bad thing. They made things to last back then. They made things that could be fixed.'

Davy's hat flung from side to side as he looked from Ralph's face back to Hendrik's. 'And you really think you can fix this?'

'I'll have a go. I have to because you and Ralph haven't got the bottle to go into the tunnel.'

'I still think you're crazy, sonny.' Mad Bill was looking down at me now because I was an elf all by myself on the bench. 'Wouldn't you rather stay on this island for Christmas? Bad enough you've married a foreign woman! Now you want to watch her give birth?'

'That's what men do these days,' Ralph said.

'See, that's why I wanted to get into the Senate? To set things right. In my day, giving birth was women's work. They should be grateful you got them into that state to start with.'

He turned and stabbed a finger towards the beacon.

'Anyway, I'm glad that thing must have died of old age. It gets me off the hook. I was starting to think I might have broken it by hiding it inside the old toilet in the pantry.'

SEVENTY
LET ME IN, YOU OLD WEASEL

IT WAS Hendrik's second big shock for the day.

First all his gold had gone.

Now he had kissed a beacon that had spent many hours secreted inside a busted toilet bowl.

When Ralph saw Hendrik's nostrils starting to flare like those of a bull about to charge, he leapt up and put himself between Hendrik and Mad Bill.

'Outta my way,' the skipper said. 'I'm really going to kill him this time.'

The old man started running towards the house as fast as his old, little legs could carry him.

Hendrik pushed Ralph aside and gave chase.

He certainly would have caught him, too, only one of Whitey's shoes came loose. Hendrik had to stop and put it back on, by which time Mad Bill had barricaded himself in the house.

Davy and Ralph followed in case they had to save the old man again. When they arrived, Hendrik was pounding on the door. 'Let me in, you old weasel,' he shouted.

SEVENTY-ONE
WHO ARE YOU CALLING GREEDY?

THEY TRUDGED BACK to the graveyard. 'Now we're really stuffed,' Hendrik said.

He held up the yellow beacon. 'I can't fix this without tools. And if he won't let us in how can I see if there's something in the basement that might help me?'

'It's your own fault,' Ralph said. 'Why did you have to threaten to kill him?'

'He provoked me, OK? I woke up this morning a rich man. Now look what he's done to me? He's humiliated me.'

'That's your own fault too,' Davy said. 'You shouldn't go around kissing objects when you don't know where they've been.'

'Can't a man be happy? Not for me either! I knew how I planned to leave this place. I was happy for you two blokes, that we now had the means for you to get home.'

Davy was beside himself with anger. 'Well, looks like you really thought that through. Not. Even if you can still fix the *they-made-these-things-to last* emergency beacon without tools, how do you propose we get inside to get the life-raft? You know we wouldn't even be in this position if you hadn't been such an idiot.'

'That's the pot calling the kettle black.' Hendrik stepped towards

Davy again. 'You were the one who spotted all that paint stored in the tunnel, but you never said it was *gold* paint. If you had, we would have twigged.'

Ralph intervened to break them up.

'Calm down, you blokes,' he said. 'I'll go see if he'll let me in at least, but it'll all be a wasted effort if you kill each other while I'm away.'

SEVENTY-TWO

LOOKING DOWN THE BARREL AGAIN

RALPH STOOD in front of the door with the feeling of déjà vu.

How many days before had he stood in this very place? Only this time he was wearing a Santa hat and he was dry. He knocked.

'Go away,' Mad Bill yelled.

'It's me. Ralph. I'm here alone.'

'Prove it.'

'How can I prove it unless you open the door and see? I give you my word though.'

The door stayed shut.

But Ralph could hear shuffling inside.

'What do you want?'

'What do you mean what do I want? I want to come in and talk this over.'

Ralph heard the lock being unlatched, and the door opened a sliver. Then he realised he was looking down the barrel of the old man's shotgun once more, and he put his hands up.

'Not this again! You must know by now you can trust me?'

The door opened wider and Mad Bill's eyes darted around until he was satisfied Hendrik wasn't there.

Ralph instinctively looked away from the gun (the thought oh being shot in the eye was unbearable) and got a good view of the skipper and Davy over at the graveyard. They were no longer at each other's throats but were seated on the bench.

Hendrik gave him a little wave. He had told Ralph exactly the kind of tool he should look for if he was able to talk Mad Bill into letting him go down to the cellar. Hendrik had said he needed something resembling a little screwdriver so he could inspect the inner workings of the beacon.

Davy had said that still didn't explain how they were going to get the life-raft but Hendrik had said they needed to take one step at a time.

Davy had said that was easy for him to say, because he planned to use a tunnel to escape.

But Hendrik had pointed out he had now been forced to change his exit plans. If the old coot would not let him back into the house, how the hell could he even access the tunnel! He was now coming on the raft, too. He'd rather incur his wife's wrath for coming home early than stay on the island with this crazy old goat.

'Can I come in and talk?'

Mad Bill finally lowered the gun.

SEVENTY-THREE
I'D BRING BACK THE CAT O'NINE TAILS FOR PEOPLE LIKE HIM

RALPH SAT DOWN at the kitchen table and tried to heal the rift with Mad Bill over several glasses of sherry. Hendrik and Davy must have been wondering why he was taking so long.

'All I want to do is check the basement to try to find the tools Hendrik needs to fix the beacon,' Ralph said.

'Phttt. I don't want nothing more to do with that joker.' Mad Bill waggled his finger at Ralph. 'He belongs in prison. You saw him trying to kill me?'

'You'd be angry, too, if you'd just kissed what he had kissed.'

'I'd bring back the cat'o'nine tails for people like him. If I can't get him off my island, at least I can keep him out of my house. And if I catch him raiding my veggie patch, he'll get lead pellets up his clacker.'

Ralph tutted. 'You don't mean that?'

Mad Bill fixed him with eyes that seemed to confirm he bloody-well did.

'It's actually in your interests to let me look for the tools he needs,' Ralph pleaded. 'Hendrik has decided to come on the life-raft with us. So if he can fix the beacon he's not going to be around here much longer.'

'Well, good riddance. I hope you and Davy make it, but I hope he drowns at sea. Or dies of scurvy. Or you have to kill him and eat him.'

'You don't mean that.'

Those confirming eyes lasered in on Ralph again.

Ralph pushed a bit harder. 'So you'll let me check out your basement? Hendrik wants me to look for a screwdriver, or something like a screwdriver.'

Mad Bill's eyes raised upwards. 'Oh, all right. You can. But it probably won't do you any good. You heard him? The beacon was already second-hand when he got it. That makes it nearly as old as my suspenders.' He twanged them. 'But these still do the job.'

'I have to trust him when he says he can fix it.'

Mad Bill blew a raspberry. 'Trust him? It was him who led those scallywags here. You must be a worse judge of character than he is.'

Ralph didn't mean to raise his voice. It just came out like that. 'It's not as if I have a choice.'

'We all have a choice, sonny. For a while there I thought I'd have people to bury me when I die. But now I just want them to leave, and that's *my* choice.' He sighed. 'It's probably for the best. I'm not sure I want to share that graveyard with Darkey anyway.'

'But what choice do I have? Hendrik is my only way off this island.'

'Is he? You sure?'

Mad Bill stood up and they walked to the top of the narrow stairs. He took a candle off the wall and handed it to Ralph.

It was only then Ralph figured out what the old man had meant. He was offering him — and him alone — a way to escape to the mainland via a tunnel.

'You don't mind if I don't come down there with you?' Mad Bill said. 'The door's not locked. I'm still looking for the key.' He looked up into Ralph's eyes. 'I can't choose for you though.'

As Ralph descended, each one of those 22 steps was like an arrow piercing his heart.

On one hand, it would be wrong of him to leave Hendrik and Davy stranded on this island with no reasonable way to escape. Sooner or later they'd run out of stinky candles and the rats would get them.

On the other hand, he knew they were resourceful men. Well, Hendrik was. But Maria needed him. He wanted to be there to welcome his daughter into this world. He needed, too, to head off any plans to hold a memorial service for him when he wasn't actually dead.

Ralph opened the door at the bottom and the first thing he saw were the tunnels. It was his chance for freedom.

He didn't know why he did it. Perhaps the sherry had gone to his head.

Ralph ran towards the same tunnel Whitey and Darkey had chosen. He was going home. Alone.

SEVENTY-FOUR
BREATHE IN, BREATHE OUT

"RUNNING" WAS probably a bit of an exaggeration. What Ralph actually did was walk with purpose.

When you are dashing into a dark tunnel that might have killer rats waiting in the shadows to gnaw on your eyeballs, you don't risk creating a draught that will blow out the candle that's the only thing protecting you from harm. The stench of the burning candle did intensify as Ralph went deeper into the confined space. But he had no choice but to take deep breaths.

Breathe in, breathe out. One step in front of the other. Just concentrate on going in the right direction. I'm coming Maria, I'm coming.

The candle trembled in his hand.

Breathe in, breathe out. Oh, that's awful! *Try not to cough and blow the candle out. Above all, watch out for rats!*

It was getting cold. His shorts and short-sleeve shirt were designed to keep a linesman comfortable as he ran up and down the sidelines. But obviously no thought had been given to keeping the wearer warm in a cold, dark tunnel.

Ralph felt grateful he was still wearing his Santa hat, which kept his head warm at least. His plan was to blow his whistle vigorously if rats attacked. That might startle them long enough for him to get away.

Ralph approached the first bend where he knew Whitey and Darkey had come to grief. Taking that first corner was probably the hardest thing he had done in his whole life. He slowed down to dead slow.

Once around the corner, he lifted the candle above his head and examined the hole in the brickwork. He moved the candle around so it could illuminate the ground ahead of him. Last thing Ralph wanted was to trip over Whitey's body. OK, not the last thing! Killer rats were still his No. 1 fear but he didn't want to come face to face with Whitey's corpse either, not that he'd be able to see anything if he had tripped over and the candle had flung free of his grip. But he couldn't think of anything worse than reaching out and feeling Whitey's cold face or, even worse, sticking a finger into an empty eye socket.

All Ralph could see ahead of him were skid marks though. No Whitey! He looked upwards again. This could only mean he was still up there, wedged in among the concrete and dirt, which could rain down at any moment. Ralph knew Hendrik and Davy were even further up there, probably sitting on the bench in the graveyard and wondering where he had got to.

Ralph felt awful again. How could he have deserted them like this?

He thought of shouting "goodbye" but he decided they'd never hear him through all that earth. And even if they did hear a noise, Davy would swear the Whitey zombie was coming alive again.

Ralph kept telling himself they'd be all right with him running out on them like this.

But who was he kidding?

He had known from the look in Mad Bill's eyes the old man meant business with that shotgun. The first time Hendrik tried to raid the veggie patch, poor Davy would have to try to remove the pellets from his backside.

He kept inching forward. He knew he had to. He knew Maria wasn't going to be waiting at the other end of the tunnel, but that was the mental image he put into his head to motivate himself to shuffle forward into the unknown.

It would be so good to see her after all these days. He'd place a hand gently on her tummy. How many kicks had he missed while he had been away?

SEVENTY-FIVE
I'M COMING MARIA, I'M COMING

RALPH CAME TO ANOTHER BEND. Who would have thought he'd be topping the fear factor of the first bend so soon?

He had *known* what might lurk around the first bend. It hadn't quite been the end of the road for Whitey and Darkey, but it was certainly the beginning of the end for them. Would the mystery of whatever lurked behind the second bend be the thing that finished *him* off?

The good thing was he had seen no rats at all.

Could it be the glow of this candle was pushing them further back into this tunnel?

Would they be waiting for him around this bend?

Ralph cocked his ear to listen for their hisses.

He heard nothing. The only sounds came from the flicker of the candle he held and his stomach, which was making some strange noises, possibly because he was squeezing his sphincter so tightly.

I'm coming Maria, I'm coming.

SEVENTY-SIX
FORKED AND FAR FROM HOME

WHAT HE SAW when he rounded the second bend was something he had never expected.

The tunnel came to a fork.

Ralph was staring at a left tunnel and a right tunnel.

Who would have thought there would be two tunnels?

He hoped one of them led to the coast, but he couldn't even think where the other one might go. The bowels of hell? Tasmania? Oh shit! What to do?

Ralph shone the candle into each tunnel in turn, but the light didn't reach far before it faded into more darkness.

He looked behind. Should he go back?

No, he might never see Maria again if he returned.

Breathe in, breathe out.

Eenie, meeny, miny, mo.

He made his choice.

He went left.

In hindsight, it wouldn't have mattered if he had gone right.

The first clue came less than 50 tentative steps into the tunnel when he came to another bend. Ralph could see from the light of the candle someone had carved their initials into the brickwork on the wall. He raised the candle for a closer look. It said *W.C (aka M.B.) Was Here.* So the old bugger had lied? He had been this far!

The bend turned acutely, giving him the sense he was now going in the direction he had come from. When the tunnel deposited him back at the fork he had started at, he knew his senses were spot on. He was headed back to where he had started!

Ralph couldn't believe it! Who knows how many years of nervous energy he had wasted in this dead-end tunnel!

What happened next was primal. He screamed as loud as he could. All he managed to achieve was to blow his candle out, which meant he had to grope his way along a wall in the dark to find his way back to the cellar.

Ralph had mixed feelings when he finally saw the flickering candle at the end of the tunnel.

He knew it wasn't Maria waiting there.

When he came out into the cellar, Mad Bill was cackling.

'You old bastard! You knew, didn't you?' Ralph said as he stomped towards him. The old man had rested a candle on the card table, and he was rocking with laughter in his chair.

He used a knuckle to wipe away his tears. 'Made you scream like a girl.'

Ralph tore off his Santa hat and threw it on to the ground. 'Why did you tell me to go?'

'At my age, sonny, you have to take belly laughs where you can get them.'

SEVENTY-SEVEN
HE'S A LYING OLD BUGGER

RALPH FELT HENDRIK'S and Davy's eyes upon him the moment he came out of the house.

As he trudged towards them, using a hand to shield his eyes from the blinding light served a dual purpose. It gave him some respite from their glare while he weighed up whether he was going to lie to them or be truthful.

They jumped up from the bench on his arrival.

Hendrik spoke first. 'Where have you been?'

'Don't ask.'

Hendrik arched his eyebrows. 'Where's the screwdriver?'

'What?'

Hendrik put a hand on Ralph's shoulder and guided him towards the bench. 'You'd better sit down. You look like you've seen a ghost!'

Davy said: 'You were in there so long we thought Mad Bill must have taken you captive. We was working out just how we could storm the house so the three of us could escape through one of the tunnels.'

Ralph was starting to shake his head before his bum even hit the seat. 'That wouldn't have done you any good.'

'He couldn't shoot us all,' Davy said. 'Maybe you? But Hendrik and I would overpower him then, and we'd be home free.'

Ralph continued to shake his head. 'The tunnel on the right doesn't go anywhere but back to where it starts.'

Hendrik's eyes widened. 'How do you know that?'

'Where do you think I've been?'

'In the tunnel?' His mind clicked through the gears. 'You were going to leave us here?'

'I was going to send help,' Ralph said. 'But Mad Bill knew it just loops back on itself.'

'But how did he know?' Davy said. 'He told us he had never been brave enough to even go into the tunnels?'

'I saw proof he's been in at least one of them. Who else would have carved his initials in the wall? What's worse, he was the one who put the idea in my head to use it to make my escape!'

'He told you to go?' Hendrik rolled his eyes.

Ralph hung his head. 'I just wanted to get home to Maria. Mad Bill thought it was a great joke.'

SEVENTY-EIGHT

YOU SAID YOU COULD MEND IT

MAD BILL HAD SUGGESTED to Ralph he might have better luck in the other tunnel but he wasn't going to be humiliated twice!

'You didn't think to look for a screwdriver?' Davy said.

'No, I just wanted to get out of the house.'

'You didn't see anything that *looked* like a screwdriver?' Davy pressed him. 'A lock pick? Anything?'

'My priorities changed, OK?'

Hendrik sat down beside Ralph, and picked up the beacon, which was sitting on the ground next to his Santa hat. 'Well, it's probably beyond fixing anyway,' he said as he examined the beacon.

'You said you could mend it,' Davy shouted.

'Does it matter now?' Hendrik said, matching the volume level. 'Now we know what a sick sense of humour he has, it wouldn't surprise me if he's in there now drilling tiny little holes in the life-raft. No way am I going to go to sea in that thing now.'

'So what's the plan now?' Davy said. 'Stay here and starve?'

'We won't starve,' Hendrik said. 'He's the one who'll run out of Rice Bubbles and snake. What's he going to have to sustain him? Sherry? Sooner or later, he's going to have to come outside and make peace with us. Then we'll have the upper hand in negotiations.'

'He might have more food in secret cupboards we never found,'
Ralph said.

'Maybe. But the good thing about us being out here is we get to
greet anyone first who comes to the island. I don't know about you,
but I don't think I've ever been more frustrated than yesterday when a
door separated us and those Navy people and there wasn't a damn
thing I could do about it.'

Davy looked at his shoes. Well, Darkey's shoes actually. 'Guess
we'll never see those people again. The thing is, they were in the right
place and didn't know it. Jesus!'

Hendrik put the beacon back on the ground.

'Don't worry, there's bound to be other visitors to the island,' he
said. 'Didn't Mad Bill say the real estate man is always coming by?'

'But how long is that going to be?' Davy kicked at the dirt.

'It's not like it's cold out here at night.' Hendrik swept his arm from
right to left. 'And we have food in abundance. We've got Mad Bill's
veggie patch on our doorstep.'

'I'd be careful there.' Ralph opened his eyes so wide they hurt. 'If
he sees you bending over near his doorstep, he'll take pot shots at you
from the window.'

SEVENTY-NINE
YOU'RE NEXT, SKIPPER

THEY DREW straws to see who'd get to sleep on the park bench.

Ralph knew Davy cheated to win, but he didn't say anything. It was only a matter of time before Davy realised the reason Mad Bill had fitted so well on the bench was that he was a head shorter than Davy and him and probably a head and a half shorter than Hendrik.

Ralph knew he'd be more comfortable sleeping on the ground anyway. Fronds from nearby trees made passable pillows.

They were lucky. They had seen where the candles were kept, and there were lots of them. Matches were in shorter supply but Hendrik said he had learnt to make fire when he was a boy scout.

'Did they actually have scouts when you were a boy?' Davy asked.

'How old do you think I am?' Hendrik said.

'Dunno.' Davy pointed to the house. 'But once he kicks the bucket, you know you'll be next in the queue.'

Hendrik balled up his fists again.

'Is anyone taking bets on that? Because if they are, I wouldn't mind a piece of the action. I'm betting you'll go before me, dickhead.'

EIGHTY
IS IT JUST ME? OR HAS THIS BENCH GOTTEN SHORTER?

THE BEACON CAME in handy after all.

Hendrik used it to smash open a golden coconut for our dinner.

It was really quite good. Not the beacon! They knew that would taste like shit. Tough too! But the coconut flesh was yummy. And the coconut milk was refreshing. It was nice to drink something other than sherry.

Mind you, Ralph was really looking forward to fish tomorrow if Davy could work out how he was going to catch them.

They hit the sack not long after the sun sank into the sea.

'I bags we swap around tomorrow night,' Davy said, as they drifted off to sleep. 'Is it just me? Or has this bench gotten shorter?'

EIGHTY-ONE
THEY'RE BACK

RALPH WAS EXHAUSTED after the day's mental drain. If he dreamed about getting off the island, he couldn't remember. He fell into a deep slumber.

He was wakened by an almighty noise and savage swirling of dust at dawn.

He lifted his head and watched a helicopter disappear over the other side of the house in murky morning light. He could hear the rotor blades powering down.

Ralph looked from Hendrik to Davy, wondering what was going on.

Hendrik scrambled to his feet excitedly. 'They're back.'

Then he started running towards the house.

'Don't do that,' Ralph yelled. 'You'll be within his range.'

But Hendrik kept running. Ralph sat up and braced for the shotgun blasts as Hendrik disappeared around the side of the house to where the veggie garden and chopper were.

Davy was sitting up on the bench. 'Even Mad Bill isn't stupid enough to take on the might of the Navy.'

'You sure it's a Navy helicopter?'

Davy nodded. 'I didn't sleep so well. So I heard it way before it got here. It looked like Navy.'

'Reckon they know about us now?'

'Guess we're about to find out.' Davy nodded towards the rapidly approaching Hendrik, who was running back towards them with two people in flying suits in close pursuit.

The man carried a clipboard and the woman had something chunky and rectangular in her hand. When she reached them, Ralph could see it was some kind of communication device.

She introduced herself. 'I'm Lieutenant-Commander Jenny Domeney and this is my co-pilot Lieutenant Jeremy Rogerson. Leading Seaman Smith is … '

She didn't finish the sentence because right then came the crack of gunshot and the ping of pellets on metal.

She got on the radio. 'Fred, what's going on? Over.'

A crackling voice replied. 'Someone's shooting at the chopper, ma'am! Over.'

'Get out of there if you can. Over.'

She put the communication device down and looked from face to face. 'Any of you gentlemen know what's going on?'

'Guess Mad Bill is crazier than we thought?' Davy said.

She gave a puzzled look. 'Who's Mad Bill?'

'He's the one doing all that shooting,' Hendrik said. 'You'd know him as William Clarin.'

Her eyes widened. 'So Captain Billycock-Smythe was right! He sent us back because he said this could be the only place left he could be.'

At that moment came the sound of smashing glass as a pellet hit home.

'At that range, Senator Clarin can do the chopper some damage,' Lt-Commander Domeney said.

Hendrik arched his eyebrows. '*Senator* Clarin? He really *is* a senator?'

'That's why we were sent to find him,' Lieutenant Rogerson said. 'He won his seat years ago but never took it up. Now, they've got a crisis on their hands and he's been elected president of the Senate in absentia on the grounds he's the only one in the chamber who doesn't carry political baggage.'

'Only he's not actually in the chamber, which is a political embarrassment,' Lt-Commander Domeney said.

'But you don't know about us?' Ralph said.

'That's what threw us,' she said. 'We had been led to believe Senator Clarin lived all alone. So when we heard your voices …'

More gunfire made more glass shatter.

'How much ammunition has he got in there? He has to run out soon, right?' Lt-Commander Domeney said.

'I wouldn't count on it,' Hendrik said. As the pings continued, he explained how they came to be on the island. He told her about the tunnels, which strangely she seemed to already know about, then he told her about Darkey and Whitey, and about their treachery and their demise. He told her how Mad Bill had locked them out and how they had lamented that they'd ever be rescued.

'You think any one of us is getting off this island in a hurry now?' she said. 'It sounds to me like the Right Honourable Senator is turning that chopper into a salt and pepper shaker.'

EIGHTY-TWO
RUSH THE HOUSE? WE'RE VERY BIG ON OCCUPATIONAL HEALTH AND SAFETY

'CAN'T YOU DO SOMETHING?' Hendrik said.

'Like what?' Lt-Commander Domeney said.

'Radio for backup?' Hendrik pointed to the communication device.

'This only reaches as far as the chopper, and I told Leading Seaman Smith to leave it. Even if I could contact someone, what would I say? That we're being bailed up by an 81-year-old senator? My superiors would have a hard time explaining to the taxpayers the saviour of the Senate had shot up several million dollars worth of helicopter.'

'So what are you saying?' Davy said. 'You're stranded on this island, too?'

She shrugged. 'Captain B.S. knew we were coming here.'

The shooting stopped.

'This is your chance,' Hendrik said. 'He's obviously run out of ammo.'

'I thought you said he had lots of ammo?' Lt-Commander Domeney said.

'He has, but he's probably had to go down to the basement to get it. This is your chance to rush the house.'

She looked at him oddly. 'Rush the house? We're very big on Occupational Health and Safety in the Navy. What if he's just foxing? What if he's at the window just waiting for someone to try to make a hero of themselves?'

EIGHTY-THREE
WE'RE TRAINED FOR SIEGE SITUATIONS LIKE THIS

THE LULL DID GIVE LEADING Seaman Smith a chance to get away.

But by the time he joined the others at the graveyard, though, the shooting had started up again with gusto.

'I tried to send out a radio message to get some back-up here, ma'am, but I couldn't get through.' Leading Seaman Smith was still puffing and wiped the beads of sweat from his forehead with a hanky he dug out of his pocket. 'We'll have to do something ourselves. That shooter is going berserk. We have to stop him or our chopper will be beyond repair.'

'The problem is he's apparently got a vast supply of ammunition,' Lt-Commander Domeney said.

'Can't we sneak up on the house? Surround him?'

'It's too dangerous.'

'He can't get all of us!'

This just made her angry. 'Calm down. That's an order, Leading Seaman!'

'I've got a plan,' Hendrik said. Lt-Commander Domeney glared at him but he seemed oblivious he was hitting another nerve by being a civilian offering a viewpoint on a matter she felt encroached on her command.

Hendrik pointed to a patch of ground between Whitey's departure point and the house. 'By my calculations, if we dig there we'll hit the top of the tunnel. We can lower someone down and they could sneak up behind Mad Bill and disable him.'

'Good plan,' LS Smith said. Then he said: 'What tunnel?'

Lt-Commander Domeney turned her glare on him. 'That's classified information.' But then she sighed. 'I guess we're at the need-to-know stage. The big question though is how exactly are we going to dig this hole?'

Hendrik pointed to the two shovels leaning against a nearby tree, where they had been left after the grave digging.

'I thought you could lower me down into the tunnel,' Hendrik said.

Lt-Commander Domeney shook her head. 'I don't think so. If anyone goes into a classified tunnel it'll be us.'

'But I know the layout of the house, you don't,' Hendrik said.

'Yes, but we've got the correct security clearance to go down there.' Lt-Commander Domeney motioned for Lieutenant Rogerson to hand over his clipboard and pen. 'Draw us a map — before you start digging.'

Ralph always thought military people were practised at digging holes, but this time it didn't seem to be the case. The three of them sat on the bench and watched Davy, Hendrik and him rotate digging shifts with the two shovels.

Most of the digging took about an hour, during which time Mad Bill hardly let up with his shooting spree. The only time the ping, ping, ping noises subsided, they heard him shout: 'You can just go back to where you come from. I don't want to buy a pock-marked helicopter.'

It took them another hour to pierce the top of the brick-lined tunnel with the crowbar, which also hadn't been put away, and at least half an hour to lower the three Navy people.

They looked down into the hole, and wished them well.

In hindsight, they should never have left their spades lying on the ground.

EIGHTY-FOUR
CAVE-IN

NO SOONER HAD the Navy personnel gone out of sight, the ground made a cracking noise.

Like a giant snake, the tunnel started opening up ahead of them in a mighty roar. In just a couple of minutes, a long stretch collapsed, sucking lots of earth and rubble into the ground.

There was nothing they could do.

'You think they're dead?' Davy said.

'Quick, we need to start digging.'

They looked around for the spades, but saw they had been sucked into the ground too.

They started digging with their bare hands. They kept at it for a good half an hour.

It's doubtful Mad Bill had heard the rockfall because as they dug desperately he kept up his ping, ping, ping.

'This is pointless,' Ralph finally said, standing up and stretching his back. 'Even if they're still alive, we don't know where to dig.'

Hendrik kept at it, and Davy had to restrain him to stop him from moving more rocks and dirt.

'But it's my fault they were down there,' Hendrik said. 'It should have been me. It was my idea.'

Ralph put a hand on his shoulder.

'Don't blame yourself. There's nothing more you could have done. We have no choice now. We'll have to wait until he runs out of ammo.'

Davy said: 'How many days do you think that will take?'

EIGHTY-FIVE

PINK AND BLACK HELICOPTER WITH WHITE BLOTCHES

THEY HAD SLUMPED on to the park bench when they heard it. The ping, ping, ping was broken up with the distant sound of another helicopter rapidly approaching .

When they stood and saw the shape getting bigger and bigger in the western sky, they started jumping up and down, and waving their arms.

'How did they find out so soon to send a rescue party?' Hendrik had forgotten his despair. Then he remembered the cave-in tragedy. 'What are we going to tell them?'

Davy was still looking up. 'Since when have Navy helicopters been black, white and pink?'

He was right. The other two looked up and saw it was close to the island now. The underside indeed was pink. The body was mainly black but it was covered in white blotches.

It passed over them, turned around at the end of the island and came in from the east to land. As it flew closer, they could see there were two people in the cockpit.

Whether the pilot saw them, Ralph didn't know. He suspected, though, no-one on board heard the gunshots or noticed the state of the other helicopter. If they had, they probably wouldn't have landed right next to it.

Not that he could see it once it fell below the rooftop, but it had to be right alongside. He could hear the engine being cut and the rotor blades slowing down.

But he could also hear something else.

Interesting fact: the ping a shotgun pellet makes when it hits a blue-grey Navy helicopter is a noticeably different noise to the ping it makes on a black, white and pink helicopter.

The shooting stopped and they heard Mad Bill's voice. 'I told you last time.'

A different voice answered. A male voice. It sounded like he said: 'Where do you want her?'

Her? That didn't make any sense!

The shooting started again. Then another gun joined in.

'That sounds like a rifle,' Hendrik said. 'Whoever they are, they're shooting back!'

More pings, more glass shattering.

Twenty minutes into the gun battle, they heard the first scream.

Ten minutes later they heard two other distinct yelps of pain almost at the same time.

Then silence.

They stood and strained to listen.

Nothing.

'What do we do now?' Davy said.

'I guess we have to get closer,' Hendrik said.

They shuffled on their bellies commando-style to the other side of the house.

They could see two men slumped in the cockpit of the black, white and pink helicopter, Hendrik opened the door and checked inside. He was shaking his head, before his head disappeared as he peered into the back.

He alighted shaking his head even more.

'Is someone else dead too?' Ralph said.

'No. But it'll be a while before that cow gives milk again. I'd say she's highly agitated.'

'There's a *cow* in the back of the helicopter?'

'You can see for yourself later. Right now, we need to check on Mad Bill.'

'You think he's dead too?'

'Either that or he's run out of ammo.'

Davy and Hendrik used a log bordering the veggie garden to smash their way through the front door, and found Mad Bill slumped in a pool of blood on the kitchen floor.

He looked up with that mischievous smile of his. His last words on this earth were: 'Told you I'd be first. You can open the envelope on the table now.'

EIGHTY-SIX
BURY ME GOOD AND DEEP

IT WAS good they knew exactly where Mad Bill wanted to be buried. It wasn't so good they didn't have the shovels any more.

'That's it, we'll have to wait until the other Navy people arrive,' Davy said. 'They've got to dig up their comrades, AND take the two bodies from the other chopper take back to the mainland. One more won't hurt.'

'We can't do that!' Ralph said. 'He wanted to be buried on this island.'

Davy scowled and raised his voice. 'He wanted to kill the skipper too!' He looked to Hendrik for support.

'That he did, but ...'

'But what?' Davy said.

'But we should respect his final wishes. It's not like we've got anything else to do now.'

Davy looked at Ralph as if he were mad. 'Didn't you say he had changed his mind? That he didn't want to be buried alongside Darkey?'

'I don't think he really meant that.' Ralph waved the will. 'He certainly didn't change the wording of this.'

'He obviously didn't get the chance with everything going on like it did,' Davy said.

'We buried Darkey after everything he allowed Whitey to do to us. Giving Mad Bill a decent send-off is the least we can do.'

Davy flicked back his hair. 'You blokes have gone soft.' Then he sighed. 'Well, if I have to make another coffin, you blokes are definitely doing the digging — shovels or no shovels.'

EIGHTY-SEVEN

SIX VOICES, ONE MOO AND A FUNERAL

AS IT TURNED OUT, they found two more shovels in the basement. They also found three Navy personnel, who were very happy when the door was opened.

They hadn't died in the cave-in, after all, though they had had to quicken their pace as the tunnel started collapsing behind them. When they reached the main chamber, and dusted themselves off, they found the door was locked from the other side.

The noise told them that something else was going on upstairs. Another helicopter? The distinct sound of another gun! Shouting! Screams! It was frustrating not being able to do anything.

When everything had gone quiet, they stopped guessing about what was going on and tried to work out how they were going to get out of there.

Were they glad to see Ralph, Hendrik and Davy!

They were made to pay for their freedom though.

They had to take their turns on the shovels to dig the grave in exactly the spot Mad Bill had wanted. Then their logistics expertise was called on to unload the cow from the black, white and pink helicopter.

It took all six of them to carry the large coffin from the basement up to the kitchen. When they opened the lid to lift his body in they saw why it was so heavy. Carpenter Davy had already half-filled it with the gold-painted iron bars.

The actual funeral was better than anything Mad Bill had planned. Six people, one cow and the Australian flag fluttering nearby would have excelled his dreams.

The six of them even sang. It wasn't so much six-part harmony but six different melodies punctuated by the odd moo. The only thing missing was a 21-gun salute for the dearly departed new president of the Senate but they had heard enough gunfire anyway.

EIGHTY-EIGHT

MAD TO THE END, SILLY OLD BUGGER

RALPH WOKE UP when dawn's light tipped through their bedroom window.

Hendrik and Davy were still snoring, and Ralph couldn't hear anyone else, which probably meant the Navy people were still asleep in their rooms. He dressed quietly and crept downstairs.

Ralph shuddered when he saw the broken front door again. Who knows what vermin had just waltzed right in during the night! Maybe he should move his bed back to the graveyard? It was getting crowded there, for sure, but as the rats and the snakes took over the house, it was probably going to be a safer place to sleep.

Lt-Commander Domeney was optimistic they wouldn't have too many nights left on this island though.

The radios in both choppers had been all shot up but she said she hoped Captain Billycock-Smythe would send a helicopter to search for them once he realised they hadn't returned.

Lt-Commander Domeney had let it slip after her fifth glass of sherry last night that she didn't have the greatest faith in the captain. He had arrived at the base unannounced one day and said he was on exchange from the Royal Navy.

As Ralph walked towards the graveyard to say good morning to

Mad Bill, he thought of Maria and the baby. As he stood at the foot of the old man's grave, watching birds pick at the freshly turned soil, he thought only good things about him. Mad to the end.

When he started back towards the house, he smiled when he realised his job at the newspaper was probably gone. His stingy employers would probably never accept the excuse he had for missing the mayor's birthday party.

His thoughts were upturned when he heard the now-familiar buzz in the distant west and looked out to the horizon.

The speck got bigger rapidly as it came towards him.

With the rising sun at his back, he could see the blue-grey helicopter. It circled the island and approached from the east. It felt so good to feel the downdraft as it passed over his head.

Ralph ran to where it landed, next to the other clapped-out choppers.

The co-pilot was first to get out. He introduced himself as Lieutenant Kim Nguyen. Was Ralph glad now Mad Bill wasn't there to see the first Asian-Australian arrive on the island!

EIGHTY-NINE
SEAMAN SMITH STAYS BEHIND WITH THE COW

THERE WASN'T room for the six of them and the cow and the two dead visitors in the rescue helicopter. Leading Seaman Smith was ordered to stay on the island and guard the corpses and the cow.

'We'll be back for you,' Lieutenant Nguyen reassured him.

Hendrik added: 'If you get hungry, there are plenty of boxes of breakfast cereal in the house. Ever milked a cow?'

Ralph was mightily glad when they lifted off. He glanced out the window and was surprised to see a white rabbit hopping near the graveyard. It must have been a trick of the light. It must have been a rat, surely?

Soon he could see mainly only sea out the window. The island now was just a speck when he craned his neck.

Everything had worked out for the best.

Mad Bill was where he wanted to be.

Whitey and Darkey probably weren't in the places they wanted to be but they were in the places most of the rest of them wanted them to be.

Democracy had probably dodged a bullet by Mad Bill not becoming president of the Senate. Ralph could only imagine the commotion he'd have caused among security guards when the metal detector at the entrance to Parliament House in Canberra started beeping madly the first time he arrived for work with his shotgun secreted in his luggage.

'*You can't bring that in here, sir.*'

'*Why not? How else do you expect us to get that piece of legislation through?*'

Ralph tried to put the thought out of his head.

He tried to get the focus on him.

First thing he wanted was a shower.

And some clean clothes would be wonderful. He had never worn his linesman outfit for more than a few hours but he had been wearing this clobber now for nearly a week.

When he ran his hand over the whiskers on his face, he realised he hadn't seen a mirror for days.

Despite five of them being in the back of the chopper, there wasn't a lot of conversation during the 30-minute flight back to the Naval base. Ralph guessed they were all thinking of being reunited with loved ones.

He knew Maria wouldn't be there waiting for him next to the helipad. She probably still thought he was dead. That wasn't the Navy's fault. They hadn't known exactly who they were rescuing until they rescued them.

But Ralph knew how the media worked. They always had their ear to the ground. It wouldn't surprise him to step out of the helicopter into a waiting media pack poking their cameras and microphones and phone recording devices at him. Wouldn't that be a weird feeling being on the other side of the media spotlight! It's definitely not what he wanted. He didn't want Maria's first glimpse of him to be a dishevelled figure on the 6.30 News. She didn't need the shock, her being in the state she was.

NINETY

THE BRITISH NEVER TOLD US

RALPH WAS WRONG. The only people waiting for them wore white protective suits and they quickly ushered them into what he later learned was a sealed-off wing of the base hospital.

There they were examined by various doctors wearing similar attire.

The doctors asked lots of questions about what they had done on the island, what they had eaten, what they had drunk, and how they were feeling.

They let them shower and shave, and gave them gowns and clean underwear but then they made them lie in beds and proceeded to prod them with thermometers and look down their throats and make them say "arrh", and take samples of their blood, saliva and urine.

'What's going on?' Ralph asked the oldest-looking of the fresh-faced doctors. 'I need to get home to my wife.'

'The captain will answer all your questions when he comes in tomorrow.'

'Tomorrow? You don't understand! My wife is heavily pregnant. She needs me.'

'We need to keep you in for observation for a few days.'

Captain Jeremy Billycock-Smythe did come and see them, but not until two days later. He was a tall man who spoke with a clipped English accent.

By this time, they were well fed, well rested and feeling just fine.

'When can we go home?' Ralph demanded.

'No need to get angry, old boy,' Captain B.S. said. 'Things will happen in the fullness of time.'

He twiddled his moustache. 'It's quite worrying to us that you've been inside that tunnel. The British hierarchy never told us why they built the tunnel or what they used it for or stored in it.'

He let out a lungful of air in a long, noisy blast. 'And as for poking around in that old graveyard? We have absolutely no idea what disease caused people to be sent to that island. We can only assume it was highly contagious. Whether that contagion still lives in the soil around the graveyard is anyone's guess!'

'Can't you take samples of the soil?' Ralph said.

'Are you crazy? I have no intention of sending anyone back to that island. Too damn dangerous.'

'But when can we go home?' Ralph asked again.

'That's up to the doctors, old boy. But I would think it'll only be a matter of weeks. If they're happy, you ought to be home early in the new year.'

'New year! Maria is due to give birth on Christmas Day!'

Captain B.S. shook his head. 'You should be thanking me. I'm giving you an out. Jesus wept, the delivery room is no place for a man.'

The Navy did get in touch with Maria to at least let her know Ralph was still alive.

She became a regular visitor but it was hard to hear what she was saying with that clear plastic screen between them.

Her belly had grown enormous. How he longed to be able to hug her, but they had to be happy just to talk.

They talked for hours about their love for each other, their plans and their fears.

Hendrik expressly asked that Madge not be contacted. He wanted to surprise her by turning up on Christmas Day with two crayfish. He told Ralph he couldn't wait to see the look on her face when he burst in and announced: 'Honey, I'm home!' He was also curious to find out how much money she had spent honouring him with the memorial service.

Davy said he didn't want anyone contacted either, especially the tattoo studio where he still owed money. Come to think of it, he said, it would be better for his economic health in several places if everyone thought he was dead.

All the Navy people were moved to another wing of the hospital after a couple of weeks. This made no sense to Ralph knowing they had been in the same tunnel and digging in the same gravesite. But he guessed they got upgraded to nicer officers' digs.

He never saw LS Smith at all. If Captain B.S. was fair dinkum about it being too treacherous sending anyone back to the island, he could only assume he was still there. But at least he had a cow to watch him bury those other corpses.

Maria was really the only link to the outside world for all three of them left in the isolation ward.

She was able to fill them in about Whitey and Darkey. Apparently, they had escaped from prison together. They had managed to botch the only bank job they had had time to do before Hendrik had encountered them in that dark back bar.

Maria also heard on the news something about the two men who had arrived with the cow. As they had suspected, one was the breakfast cereal salesman. Coincidentally, he might have known Whitey and Darkey because they had been in the same prison together.

The pilot was the real estate agent, who had recently traded in his sleek new yacht and upgraded to a helicopter that he had had painted in the black, white and pink livery of his agency. As far as anyone knew, he didn't have a criminal record so how he teamed up with the dodgy breakfast cereal salesman was a mystery that died with him on Mad Bill's Island.

NINETY-ONE
GET ME TO THE BIRTH ON TIME

THEY DISCHARGED Ralph on Christmas Eve. They gave him his freshly laundered clothes to change back into.

He tried to phone Maria from the hospital with the good news he had been released early, only to be told she had already gone into labour.

What could he do? He had no car. He had no money.

He hitched a lift down the coast on a long-distance lorry.

What the driver thought of picking up a guy dressed in shorts, a red-and-black striped shirt and with a whistle around his neck, who knows?

Ralph was just thankful he got him to the maternity hospital on time.

Five minutes after Ralph got there, little Eva was born.

NEXT IN THE SERIES

FUNNY CAPERS DOWNUNDER #3

Major B.S. doesn't have a clue what the British were doing on Mad Bill's Island in World War 2. All he knows in this black comedy is he wants to get off the island. He's going to have to discover the secret the hard way.

This novella wraps up the Funny Capers DownUnder series. Guess who makes a surprise appearance? They would have known he was still alive if they had licked him!

ABOUT THE AUTHOR

JOHN MARTIN is an Australian. He used to be a journalist, now he's free to be frivolous.

https://johnmartin-author.blog

AUTHOR'S NOTE

I WROTE *Daddy's Great Escape* for NaNoWriMo (National Novel Writing Month) in November 2016. I went through my calendar and worked out what days of the month I was available, then divided the days. It meant I had to write 2500 words on those available days to meet the 50,000 word target.

It was a fun challenge. When I started, I had the first page in my head and no more. So I was writing into the dark. I normally write that way anyway but I usually have a vague idea where I'm going, and I pause about 30,000 words in to do some actual plotting. Not here though! It was 2500 words. Sleep. Wake Up. Get another 2500 words down and hope they gel.

Needless to say, it took me one month to write the first draft and the next three months to knead it into shape. And I needed another month to spruce it up for its relaunch as part of the Funny Capers DownUnder series.

In the re-editing, I changed it from first-person to third-person with a single perspective.

A HUMBLE REQUEST

If you enjoyed this novel, please leave a short review at *your favourite retailer* and/or *Goodreads.*

Reviews provide social proof of a book's worth. They help me a lot because I'm a little independent author without the backing of big promotional machines.

Your feedback helps me learn too. That's how my books can get better.

HELP ME

This novel has been professionally edited. If you've got this far my guess is you've successfully navigated the Australian spelling, slang and deliberate oddities. But typos always manage to slip through the net, so by all means let me know if something's out of order.

– John Martin
https://johnmartin-author.blog

MY BOOKS

Windy Mountain series

Lie of the Tiger (#1)

He's not who he says he is. Who will rescue him?

———

Blokes on a Plane (#2)

Why is the mayor speaking old English? And where has he disappeared to?

———

Whitey and the Six Dwarfs (#3)

Troupe of Elvis impersonators come to the rescue.

———

Blokes in Donegal (#4)

Three old blokes go to Ireland hoping to discover family history. The mayor had to take his great, great, great grandfather's head, didn't he!

———

Blokes in the House (#5)

How the old blokes coped with COVID quarantine (clue: the major didn't).

———

Who Knew Tasmanian Tigers Eat Apples. (#6)

Back to before the beginning. Wish-Wash leads a public revolt.

———

Who Knew Tiger Sharks also Eat Apples? (#7)

A character from the old days returns in an unlikely guise. It's all about comic revenge.

———

The Life and Deaths of Billy Gumboots (#8)

'His foot, my boot.'

Blokes Send in the Clones (#9)

Two old blokes have a crack at cloning a Tasmanian tiger.

To come:

10 — Blokes do the Block

Someone marries, someone dies. Might even be the same old bloke.

———

Funny Capers DownUnder series

The Wrong Magician (#1)

This time he has to make himself disappear.

———

Daddy's Great Escape (#2)

If Mad Bill hates people so much, why does he make it so hard for them to leave his island?

———

Escape from Mad Bill's Island (#3)

He came seeking to find out what the British were up to on the island in World War 2. He won't like the answer.

———

Standalone novels

Major B.S. comes to the end of his Rope

It all started when he rescued the wrong group of people from a prisoner-of-war camp. It just becomes worse.

———

www.ingramcontent.com/pod-product-compliance
Lightning Source LLC
Chambersburg PA
CBHW050421260626
47156CB00003B/1106